"It's none of your business!"

Judith said, twisting and tugging until her arm was free of his grip. "How I choose to handle my daughter is my affair. Don't worry, though. I'll see to it that she doesn't bother you again!"

"Come on, Judith! It's not that. I'm not concerned for myself, it's her. She needs a man in her life, somebody she can depend on, somebody more than that fat toad Gilly! She needs the same kind of man you need, a man who can spend the proper time and attention..."

"How dare you!" She wrenched herself free and stepped back, anger bringing new strength and rashness. "How dare you make those kinds of judgments! How would you know what I need, what my daughter needs? I'll tell you something. We don't need any man. Someday we may *want* a man, Nolan, but we don't *need* one. Least of all an arrogant, self-centered man like you!"

Dear Reader,

Although our culture is always changing, the desire to love and be loved is a constant in every woman's heart. Silhouette Romances reflect that desire, sweeping you away with books that will make you laugh and cry, poignant stories that will move you time and time again.

This year we're featuring Romances with a playful twist. Remember those fun-loving heroines who always manage to get themselves into tricky predicaments? You'll enjoy reading about their escapades in Silhouette Romances by Brittany Young, Debbie Macomber, Annette Broadrick and Rita Rainville.

We're also publishing Romances by many of your all-time favorites such as Ginna Gray, Dixie Browning, Laurie Paige and Joan Hohl. Your overwhelming reaction to these authors has served as a touchstone for us, and we're pleased to bring you more books with Silhouette's distinctive medley of charm, wit and—above all—*romance*. I hope you enjoy this book, and the many stories to come.

Sincerely,

Rosalind Noonan
Senior Editor
SILHOUETTE BOOKS

ARLENE JAMES
Now or Never

Silhouette *Romance*

Published by Silhouette Books New York

America's Publisher of Contemporary Romance

To Mary Judith Eidelmann Eichblatt,
who loves her friends and her family so well
that I've forgotten which I am!

d.a.r.

SILHOUETTE BOOKS
300 E. 42nd St., New York, N.Y. 10017

Copyright © 1985 by Arlene James

Distributed by Pocket Books

ISBN: 0-373-08404-8

First Silhouette Books printing December 1985

10 9 8 7 6 5 4 3 2 1

America's Publisher of Contemporary Romance

Printed in the U.S.A.

ARLENE JAMES

grew up in Oklahoma and has lived all over the South. In 1976 she married "the most romantic man in the world," and since then "every trip with him has been a romance to remember forever." We think you will feel the same way about her books.

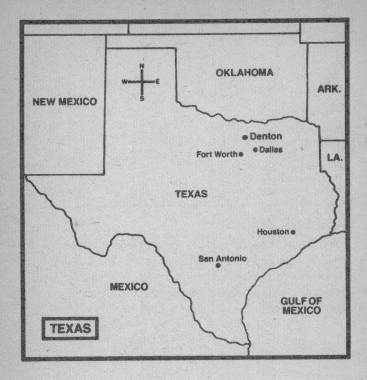

Chapter One

Nolan shouldered open the front door, the weight of the box balanced in his arms. The door crashed back against the wall, the heavy plate of etched glass shuddering in its old wood frame. Nolan shook his head, as irritated with his new landlady as with himself. That door was nearly seventy years old. An eighty-nine-cent doorstop would help protect it against breakage by fools such as himself, but the owner had never bothered to install one. Likewise, it had been a very long time since the glass had been puttied tight in the frame. He sighed. A couple of dollars plus a half hour's work and a valuable antique would be rendered safely serviceable for a number of years. Fools. The world was fairly bulging with them, and he the biggest of all.

On that glum note, he nudged the door closed with his knee and turned back toward the staircase. It was a majestic piece of architecture. Situated against a major load-bearing wall to the far right of the immense foyer, it swept upward in a wide, gentle curve to a narrow landing, its juncture in the exact center of the foyer. Both stairs and graceful banister were stained a dark, murky color.

If this were his house, he would paint the risers of the stairs and the support posts of the banister a soft candlelight white, then varnish and polish the stretchers and banister itself until they shone in the light of a crystal chandelier, which he would hang directly over that juncture with the landing. Then, in that long, narrow hallway which opened on the far left corner, he would rip up the old colorless carpet and install parquet salvaged from the foyer floor, which he would replace with marble. It would be stunning...if this were his house...if this were his house and he had the money to do what could be done, which he didn't.

Money. Money lost. Prestige lost. Honor...all lost, and Nolan Tanner was reduced to a room in a boardinghouse. Boy wonder, builder, respected architect, son of one of the wealthiest men in Dallas, living in a boardinghouse in the small city of Denton, Texas, a college town forty miles or so from his past. Indeed, Nolan Tanner, the successful businessman, existed only in his past, but he would resurface in the future, and the future would one day be the present. That he vowed. He would have it all again, the money, the thriving business, the home of his dreams, respect, all the success he had once thought his. He would again be a wealthy man, and then his father could darn well choke on his I-told-you-sos.

Meanwhile, let the world wonder where he had gone. There were a few, perhaps, who knew he had taken on this remodeling job in Denton, but they couldn't know that he was doing the actual hands-on work himself this time, not just drawing up the plans and subcontracting the labor. Let them wait and wonder what had become of him. He'd show up one day with money in his pocket and a big development cooking, and they'd all know Nolan Tanner was back on the scene. He'd like to see his father's face when that happened, like to know how he felt about his worthless son rising up out of the ruins of a crumpled empire like the proverbial phoenix. It was the day he worked for, lived for, the day he was again a wealthy man. Until then, he would do whatever it took.

Mary Judith smoothed the wall with her hand and stepped back. She hoped he would like the new paper. It brightened the room with its shades of pale coral and neutral beige, and the wheat pattern superimposed on the narrow, widely spaced stripes of pale silvery green were masculine and yet not overpowering or heavy.

She wished there was something else she could do to lighten the room. It was long and narrow, not her best room, to be sure, but spacious and comfortable with a small window that opened onto the front veranda on the north and a larger one on the west which was shaded by that big old hickory. That was a bonus this time of year in Texas. The tail end of summer was always the hottest, and anything that blocked the sun was welcome. But it did make for a gloomy room, and she sensed that Mr. Tanner was gloomy enough without any help from his surroundings.

The crash of the door against the wall reminded her that she needed to do something about it, but as always, she promptly forgot. Hurrying to the one good easy chair in the room, she plumped the cushions, swept away an imaginary speck of dust and turned swiftly, checking to make certain that all was in order.

Fresh towels hung on the rack in the small, gleaming white bathroom. Clean linens covered the high, old-fashioned double bed that stood against the newly papered east wall. The new cover she had sewn for the sofa coordinated well with the new paper and curtains. The cobwebs had been swept from every corner, and the closet had been emptied of every vestige of the previous occupant. The old refrigerator in the corner behind the door was clean and smelled of lemon, and the deep boxy shelves that passed for cabinets were freshly painted and lined with new paper. She had even managed to repair the cord on the old hot plate that served as cookstove in the tiny "kitchen," not that it was necessary for her boarders to cook much for themselves. Evening meals were served family-style in the dining room—once the living room—across the foyer next to her own private quarters.

Everything seemed in order. It was then that she heard the scritch in the lock and hurried across the room to throw open the door and greet her new guest. His reaction was hardly what she had expected. He stood looking at her with a bewildered wrinkle on his brow, a lock of coal black hair slashing the sun-browned skin of his forehead like a thick stroke of black ink on parchment. The wide brown eyes, almost too exotic and thick-lashed to belong to a male face, glared at her as if demanding to know what she was about.

"M-Mr. Tanner." That glare unnerved her. It had a touch of accusation in it. She put a hand to her tightly curled biscuit-brown hair. "I was just checking to be certain that everything was ready for you. Here, let me help.'' She reached out to take part of the weight of the box from him, but he pushed past her with apparent ease to the drop-leaf table situated at the back of the sofa and deposited the heavy box, the muscles of his forearms bulging against the knitted bands of his shirt sleeves.

He wasn't as big as he had seemed at that first meeting. He stood only an inch or two over six feet. Odd that she should have remembered him as being as tall as the door. Perhaps those wide shoulders and long muscled limbs were what made him seem so imposing. On the other hand, it could be those dark, brooding good looks. No, it was something else entirely, something about the mouth. There was a tautness about the wide spare lips, a grimness that denoted—what? Bitterness, perhaps. Stubbornness almost certainly. And pain? Yes. Very raw, like a scrape beneath the shield of a bandage. The spare mouth turned downward, and she dropped her gaze, suddenly aware that she had been staring.

He glanced about the room dispassionately. ''Everything seems fine,'' he pronounced. ''You can go now.''

Mary Judith bristled at the tone of dismissal. She was the proprietess of this establishment, not his personal maid. She lifted her chin and fixed him with an unapologetic stare.

''You do that very well,'' she told him; then, in answer to the lift of a pair of slender, arrogant brows, ''give orders, I mean.'' The brows arched higher. She folded her arms beneath high ample breasts. ''You sound as if you've had a good deal of experience with servants. Now I can't help wondering about that, can

I?'' She looked him over blatantly from head to toe, noting the longish style of his hair, expertly cut, the fashionable logo on his shirt, the designer jeans, the expensive double-last running shoes. What was he doing in a place like this?

To her surprise, the taut mouth curved upward ever so slightly. He hooked his thumbs into the waistband of his jeans and struck a casual pose against the edge of the table, his legs crossed at the ankles.

"All right, Mrs. Vickers, I was short with you. I apologize, but frankly it's been a lousy morning and I'm not exactly in the best of moods. Satisifed?"

Mary Judith inclined her head. "No," she replied flatly, "but then your moods are your own affair."

With that she turned and quickly left him, as cool— seemingly—as a cucumber. In actuality, the man "bothered" her in a way no other had in a very long time, so much so that she felt an urgent need to get away from him in order to restore the calm beneath the veneer. She wondered again what he was doing there. She was proud of what she had made of this house. It was not her first choice, of course, but how many other women in her position had done as well? Still, a boardinghouse was hardly the sort of place one expected to find a man like Nolan Tanner. Why, she mused, had she even let him have the room when there were dozens of eager college students desperate for off-campus accommodations? She pushed that question away unanswered, but a strange fluttering queasiness in the pit of her stomach would not let her put Nolan Tanner completely from mind, not for some time to come.

Nolan stared at the old-fashioned paneled door through which Mrs. Vickers had passed. He had been rude to her, and he hadn't meant to be, but it was probably just as well. She was an attractive woman, his landlady. Nice shape, good legs, neat appearance. He liked that natural look. Oh, the hair had probably been permed, all those uniform little curls clinging to her face, neck and shoulders, but she hadn't altered the color. That warm sandy brown was as genuine as the pert nose and the full, sensuous mouth. She wasn't one of those walking mannequins, all grease paint and goop. He didn't think she even wore makeup. She didn't need to with that creamy skin and those enormous gold eyes ringed with thick brown lashes.

He wondered, not for the first time, about her husband. He hadn't yet met the man, not that it mattered. From what he'd seen, he doubted they'd have much in common. He wondered, in fact, how a man who could attract a woman like that could let so many little things go unattended around here. To Nolan it just made good sense to keep up one's possessions. They were investments, after all, especially something as large and expensive as a house, even a very old one left over from the Victorian era. Actually the old place had a lot of charm about it, with its wide veranda and thick white columns and dormer windows. All the more reason to keep the place up. Besides, a man's home was something in which he ought to take pride.

However, Mary Judith Vickers and her husband were no concern of his, though he admitted it was just as well that she was married. She was an attractive woman, gutsy little thing, spunky. He liked that. But heaven knew he didn't need any more complications in his life just then, especially not of the female sort. He had other fish to fry. Specifically, he had bills to pay, creditors to satisfy, a reputation to salvage, a business to rebuild; and he'd be damned if he wouldn't do it.

Determinedly he turned his mind to matters of import. Tomorrow he could put in a full day on the remodeling job. Another couple weeks and what had once been a home very much like this one, though not nearly so large, would become a particularly charming and unique office building, the branch office of Christian, Haws, Carter and Carter, attorneys at law.

He'd always gotten along well with Boyd Carter. The two of them had a lot in common. Boyd's father was as much a problem in his own way as Nolan's was. Despite the old man's arrogance and his penchant for rumor-mongering, Boyd would never kick a man when he was down or judge him without all the facts, so Nolan hadn't been surprised when the successful young lawyer had approached him about redesigning and converting an old house into an office building. Boyd had explained that the firm wanted to open a branch office in Denton, which was the county seat of Denton County, but that the budget was slim. What he hadn't said but Nolan had intuitively known was that he was doing it with his own personal funds simply to get out of the office he shared with his father. Nolan could identify strongly with his motivation. He often wondered why Boyd had joined his father's firm in the first place. Camden Carter was an irascible, snobbish old gossip.

Nolan was pleased to be able to help Boyd. The circumstances made the deal mutually satisfying. Boyd needed a contractor with a number of talents, one who could visualize the necessary changes, design them and build them, one who knew materials and sources and had an eye for style. A conventional contractor would have brought in an independent architect, hired sub-contracted labor, offered materials available only through local outlets and charged a hefty fee for his services. In all probability he would never have picked up a hammer or taken a measurement himself. An ordinary contractor's purpose was to coordinate and intermediate.

Nolan, on the other hand, was able to do every phase of the actual work himself. He was architect, carpenter, purchaser and gofer all in one. He was able, therefore, to do the job cheaper than any conventional contractor, which aided Boyd, and the money he earned kept him fed and sheltered while he was dispensing of his personal property in an effort to pay off company debts.

When his house sold it was time to look for other living quarters, and he'd decided on Denton simply because that was the location of the job. Rent was substantially cheaper, the traffic problem was virtually eliminated because he was no longer driving the thirty or so miles along Interstate 35E to and from North Dallas, and there was the added bonus of comparable anonymity. Few people in Denton knew anything about his business difficulties. Even those who vaguely recognized his name failed to connect him with the news reporters that had set the Dallas business establishment abuzz with speculation and conjecture. In Denton he was just another working stiff trying to make a buck. In Dallas he was the dupe, the guy who fell in a cesspool and came up clean but smelling to high heaven.

Still, Denton was a rapidly growing community, close enough to Dallas to participate in the economic boom, far enough to have a distinct personality of its own. There were ample opportunities here for a man like himself. New apartment complexes were springing up all over town. Light industry was coming in at an impressive rate. An elite residential district was rapidly evolving. And a major series of new shopping centers and office buildings were under construction on the outskirts of the city.

In addition one could see an evident movement to balance all this new building by preserving the old. Denton possessed a wealth of stately old homes and commercial structures. It had become fashionable in the old, established sections of town to refurbish and redecorate. Yes, any way a body looked at it, there was money to be made in Denton, big money for the right man, and that man would be held in high esteem by the Dallas business establishment. Nolan was determined that he was going to be that man. Denton was his gateway to North Dallas, his passage home. The last thing he needed were any entanglements that might impede his progress, any hitches in his plan.

Tomorrow he would work as usual on the renovation job for Boyd. On Wednesday he was meeting with another prospective client, and the job, which was much larger and more involved, looked highly promising. Then there was that meeting with the bank in Dallas on Thursday to schedule a repayment plan for the remaining portion of a company loan about to go into default. Friday had been dedicated to a conference with the subcontractors who still had outstanding claims. He had good news for them. Since the deal had been closed on the sale of his house, he could now start settling some of those accounts. Saturday and Sunday he expected to spend at his drawing table working on plans for the new renovation job. He had a long week laid out. He would have to work evenings as well as the weekend, but so be it. He expected to have a lot more of those before he was back where he wanted to be.

If all went as he planned, he would be ready to start over again, clean, in only a few months. They would be hard months, to be sure, but months—not years. He would again be in a position to secure financing, and in the meantime he would have established a local reputation as a builder.

Two years, he told himself. *Two years at the outside and I'll be back on top!* That ought to stick in his old man's craw. He'd done it without his father before, and he would do it again, only bigger and better this time and on his own turf. One day he'd be wealthier than even Morgan Tanner, and no one could say that the prestige of the Tanner name had had anything to do with it. One day Morgan Tanner would have to admit that his son was as big a man as him, or bigger.

Nolan looked down at his hands. They had curled into steely fists of determination so tight that they ached. Instantly he relaxed them and lifted his gaze to again scan the room that was to be his temporary home. It was not so bad really. It was bright and clean and decorated with taste and style. He supposed Mrs. Vickers was responsible for that and hoped he hadn't inadvertently insulted her with his initial lack of enthusiasm. It was only that he still couldn't quite believe it was all gone; the lavish home with the kidney-shaped pool he'd built for himself in trendy North Dallas, the Persian rugs, the brass sculptures, the second car, the weight room and all that high-tech video and audio equipment.

He stepped to the table and lifted the lid on the box, surveying its contents. Here was all he'd brought with him other than his clothing and toilet articles and a few dishes. Here was all he'd saved, except a drafting table and some supplies to be delivered later: a few hardback books, a trio of ashtrays, brass bookends in the shape of rearing horses, a small wood case filled with elementary drafting tools, an automatic coffee maker and a gold-rimmed porcelain mug with his name on it. This was it, the sum total of his worldly possessions outside the realm of absolute necessities.

He picked up an ashtray, feeling its weight. Now why had he bothered about these? He didn't even smoke. Well, maybe he could use them for door-stops. Sure, he could use one to prop open the closet door and one to prop open the bathroom door, with one left over. The irony struck him cruelly, and he pushed the thing onto the table, suddenly wanting to be rid of it.

Miserable, he dragged himself over to the bed and dropped down on it. The mattress was firm and smooth, and the spread smelled of lemon and sunshine. It made him think of Mary Judith Vickers. She must have washed these sheets, made this bed. Pity, a woman like that stuck in a boardinghouse. And this could still be a fine home, too. They probably didn't even see its potential. He raised up on his elbows and looked around the room again. No, he'd bet *she* saw the possibilities.

She had obviously done the best she could with what she had. In fact the room was rather charmingly done. He wondered what her story was, why she'd con-

sented to this arrangement, taking strangers into her
home. He shook his head. Curiosity had killed the cat,
hadn't it? Better not to even wonder about other people's business. Besides, he reminded himself sternly,
she's a married woman. It was downright silly how
much relief he felt just at the reminder. It was as if
he'd been removed from harm's way, as if a potential
danger had been averted, as if he'd escaped possible
doom. But why on earth should she make him feel that
way?

He had no answer, so he simply wouldn't think
about it, he told himself. In fact, for one lazy afternoon he wouldn't think about anything. For a few
quiet hours he would do nothing, nothing at all. It
would be his latest hiatus, his lull before the storm, a
sort of minivacation away from the pressures and
troubles. Peace of mind, that was what he wanted.
One short afternoon of peace of mind. One very short
afternoon.

Texas in August means 110 in the shade. Nolan sat
on the wide front porch in a metal fan-backed chair
that needed a coat of paint and thought how glad he
was that he'd kept in shape, hadn't gone soft like so
many men who make the transition from hourly la-
borer to contractor. It had been years since he'd
worked out-of-doors in the hot summertime, but he'd
never been one to sit for long behind a desk in an air-
conditioned office. That was one thing for which he
had to thank his father, all those summers he'd worked
on construction crews, learning the business from the
ground up.

He'd learned, all right. He'd learned that he had a
real love for doing things with his own hands. He'd

learned that he had a talent for visualizing what his hands could build, that there was artistry in what so many people considered mere labor. His father had been right to insist that he experience firsthand the actual construction of a building. How ironic that it was this experience that was now his means of salvaging his life, for to Nolan his pride was his life.

He sat in the shade of the porch, enjoying the heat and listening to the prattle of the wind-rippled leaves of two enormous old trees, one a hickory, the other a sycamore. Up and down the wide street, their neighbors murmured in reply. It really was a lovely street, peaceful, even elegant in a nostalgic way. There was something compelling about these big old houses. They had a dignity about them, a certain kind of solidity even when in a state of disrepair. They sat like a double row of elders, grandmothers and grandfathers in that time of life when, despite the aches and pains of old age, the body is still stout and the lines and sags of experience and wisdom decorate weathered faces.

Perhaps it was the present insecurity of his own life, but for some reason he found a kind of continuity and security in the dignified old neighborhood. That feeling washed over him in gentle eddies until he was totally caught up in it, the approaching car only a vague, shapeless object moving along the outer edges of his field of vision.

It was one of those sleek new automobiles with the fashionable rounded and stunted angles that slowed and pulled to the curb at the end of the walk. He watched disinterestedly as a rear door opened and a munchkin with a long black ponytail popped out. A tiny hand went up, fluttering a message to the occupants in the car. Then the door closed and the car pulled away from the curb, the girl jumping in an erratic, enthusiastic ritual of farewell. She was a cute kid, he thought absently, and wondered which house she belonged to. As if she had read his mind, she spun around and flew up the walk straight toward him, her book bag in tow.

"Hi ya'." She gave him a casual greeting as she approached.

"Hello."

He wondered if she sometimes stopped to chat with whomever happened to be sitting on the boarding-house porch before going on home, but neither stopping nor chatting was on this kid's mind. Nolan watched with furrowed brow as the ponytail bobbed right on by. A little hand came up and closed on the doorknob, and he was just about to ask if she knew one of the other tenants when that cherubic little mouth opened and out came an ear-piercing bawl.

"Mom? Mo-om!"

Mom? Nolan got up and followed her inside. Without the slightest hesitation the ponytail went bouncing up the stairs. At the landing a tiny tennis shoe struggled up and over the banister, followed by the leg of a diminutive pair of blue jeans, then she was suddenly plummeting toward the floor below, riding the banister at breakneck speed. Instinctively Nolan shot forward and dropped almost to his knees, his arms flung out to catch her. She plopped into them as handily as an olive into a martini glass, wriggling and giggling, demanding to know who had caught her. Nolan straightened, his knees weakened by the lingering fright, and a small elfin face turned up to stare at him with merry inquisition.

"Who are you?"

Nolan looked down at her, astounded by the composure reflected in those perfect little features.

"Who am *I*? The question is, who are you?"

She flicked a strand of hair out of her eye. "I'm Laine. Laine Vickers."

He nearly dropped her. She whooped and thrashed her legs, then slid down his torso until her feet touched the floor. There she stood, her tiny arms wrapped loosely about his knees, that amazingly lovely face turned up at him. She was a beautiful kid, a little bundle of perfection with a pixyish grin and long dark hair even blacker than his own. Her eyes were as big as quarters and the color of pennies, a coppery brown with a tawny radiance that unnerved him. He had the uncomfortable feeling that she was looking inside his head, seeing pictures that told her in minute detail what he was thinking. A pout turned down the edges of a plump rose-red mouth.

"I wouldn't have hurt myself," she asserted petulantly. "Really. I do it all the time."

He glared down at her. "Do you live here?"

She answered him with a grin that split her face in two parts, the upper portion consisting of a pert nose and those enormous eyes. Vickers. Laine Vickers. Of course she lived here. Dumb question, especially considering how very much she looked like her mother even with the difference in coloring. Her mother was a beauty, but this kid was going to be even more striking, thanks to that exotic coloring. He realized suddenly that he was smiling at her and quickly fashioned his features into a studied scowl.

"Do your parents know you do this?" he demanded, flipping a hand to indicate the banister. Thick dark lashes dropped over those enormous copper-colored eyes. Nolan jiggled her against his knee, prompting a reply. The child bit her lip and lifted a shoulder almost imperceptibly. "I didn't think so," he said. "Well, I suppose I'll just have to speak to your mother about this. Mary Judith is your mother, isn't she?" Even before her ponytail had stopped bobbing in affirmation, he had thought better of that idea and amended his intention. "Better yet, I'll speak to your father." It was then that she put an end to his peaceful afternoon.

"Can't," she said, turning those big amber eyes up at him. "Don't got one."

Don't got one? Nolan stared down at her, beauty in miniature, a replica of a face he'd already seen too often in his mind's eye. Mary Judith Vickers's kid, and no husband after all. The bottom dropped out of his stomach, and he knew—in that instant he *knew*—it was just a harbinger of things to come.

Chapter Two

Mary Judith dug in the soft gray-black earth and thought about Nolan Tanner. Why was she always drawn to men with that lustrous black hair? Mick had had hair like that, only blacker and thicker and a little more unruly. Mick. What a nice boy he had been. Boy? He had been twenty-five years old when he had fallen out of that blasted tree on one of his many hunting trips. They'd been married three years when it happened. Laine had been a toddler running around the house as fast as her little legs could carry her. Mary Judith sat back on her heels and allowed her mind to take her into an area of speculation never before explored.

Mick would have been twenty-nine last month. Why should she think of him as a boy? Hadn't she always thought of him as a man before? Before *what?* Or perhaps the correct question was: before *whom?* It disturbed her to think that three meetings with Nolan

Tanner had changed her perception of her late husband.

It wasn't Tanner, she told herself, not really. It was time. Yes, that was it. Time distorted itself, warped one's remembered perceptions. Perhaps she had always thought of Mick as a boy but out of respect had given him a different label and now she remembered only the label. She shook her head as the small pointed spade sliced into the earth and chopped the root system of a hardy weed. Sometimes she thought too much. She smiled to herself, feeling the sun warm the taut skin of her back through her shirt, and tried not to think about Nolan Tanner. The thoughts continued to float vaguely through her mind, unacknowledged but ever present, questions that would rise to consciousness with gentle, unintentional prodding.

Laine picked up the weed her mother had popped out of the ground and flung it amid a shower of clinging dusty pellets into a paper bag. Mary Judith pulled off a glove and ruffled her honey-brown hair, freeing it of dirt. Laine loped away, her job done, singing and talking happily to herself as she made for the sandbox beside the hedge. There she took up her own spade and pretended to carefully pop her own weeds from between the imaginary heads of red and pink flowers.

Mary Judith lifted the back of her hand to her brow and watched her daughter. Laine was a happy, secure little girl, and Mary Judith knew that was partly because she had always been able to stay home with her. Because she'd had the house, it had never been necessary since Mick's death for her to go outside of her home for work. For Laine's sake, she was thankful. Oh, there had been times when she had sorely wished that she had something more than cleaning and cooking and caring for her daughter and a quartet of boarders to keep her occupied, but the truth was that she liked the way she lived. She liked sharing her life with others. It helped to make up for the absence of real family.

It had been difficult at first, breaking the house up into five separate apartments, one for her and Laine, Mr. Tanner's "efficiency," Gilly's two rooms and the three shared by Trish and Marta. With Tanner's arrival, she had one vacancy left, the tiny handyman's apartment behind the kitchen. She hoped to fill it soon. Heaven knew she could use some help around here.

Gilly had been with her for nearly three years now; Trish and Marta only ten months. The efficiency, however, seemed to turn over continuously, and it had been weeks since she'd had a resident handyman. She couldn't understand why, really. The apartment was small, but the work wasn't particularly taxing. The problem, she supposed, was that most students needed paying jobs and, this being a college town, there was certainly no surplus of capable adults willing to take on a part-time job for room and board only. Still, they had always managed. Someone would come along. Meanwhile, she'd just have to take care of any problems as they arose.

All in all, she figured she and Laine had it pretty good. They didn't have a lot of money, but they were very rich in other ways. That was how she thought of herself as she knelt there in her garden and watched her daughter slinging sand into the air and dancing around like an Indian. She was rich, so very rich. And then another thought suddenly popped into her head and she turned her gaze toward the house.

Had Nolan Tanner ever been as rich as she? Had he felt secure and loved and valued by those who loved him? What was he doing now, she wondered. Was he looking around his one-room apartment and thankfully counting his blessings? She didn't think so. Somehow she thought Nolan Tanner had very little, had always had less than she. That idea troubled her, pained her somehow, but why should she even think of it? Why should she care if Nolan Tanner had ever known the kind of incalculable wealth she and Laine enjoyed? She was asking for trouble, dwelling on the man this way, simply asking for trouble. Frowning, she plunged her blade into the earth once again. *Mary Judith,* she told herself firmly, *sometimes you just think too much.*

But Nolan Tanner was a man who didn't leave the mind as easily as he slipped into it. Try as she might to fix her thoughts on something else, she was continually drawn back to the mental image of the tall, dark, handsome man who had recently joined her household. Even as she prepared the evening meal, she couldn't help wondering if he would come to dinner, and apparently her daughter had much the same thoughts on her mind because she set an extra place at the table for him without being told to do so.

Laine hadn't had much to say about their new boarder, though she had asked her mother for his name and repeated it thoughtfully to herself several times. Nevertheless, Mary Judith could tell that her daughter liked him, a fact that was not surprising since Laine seemed to like everyone, a trait she had learned from her mother whose warm and loving nature made her open to everyone. Being very much aware of her own feelings, however, Mary Judith had to admit that her interest in Nolan Tanner went slightly beyond the norm, and that puzzled her.

He was an attractive man, even a handsome man, but there were many of those walking around. What was it about him that piqued her interest? In truth, he hadn't been much more than civil to her on the two or three occasions when they had spoken. He had that sleek black hair that she favored in men, but she couldn't say that he really looked like Mick. He was taller and slimmer than her late husband, and his features were decidedly sharper and more defined. Mick's face had been round and boyish, always smiling, always open and honest, while Nolan Tanner seemed a man of mystery. Apparently he was a private person, a quiet man who kept to himself a good deal, and Mary Judith had had little experience dealing with that type. Was that why he appealed to her, because he was different? She silently laughed at her juvenile preoccupation and tried to put the matter out of mind while she finished the preparations for the evening meal.

As usual, Gilly was the first one to show up for dinner. Mary Judith greeted him with a rather absent smile as he settled his bulk into his customary chair at the big round table. Almost without greeting, he immediately launched into a recitation of the events of his day. This was accompanied by a lengthy but familiar list of complaints, to which Mary Judith nodded and frowned as she scooped ice into the glasses. According to Gilly, the life of a graduate student and college teacher was pure misery. He was prone to wonder aloud why he let himself be so abused by his superiors and students. Oh, and it would be so much worse when the new semester actually began! Mary Judith had to school her face against a smile, for she knew that he spent the majority of his day with his feet propped up somewhere, mulling over imagined as well as real inequities in the life which he had clearly chosen for himself.

Fortunately Trish soon came in to pump new life into the conversation. She was excited about her fall courses and eager to begin the semester. She had a part-time job at the student center this year and her boss, who was an unmarried graduate student, was *so* cute. Trish, who was small and slender and had long yellow-blond hair, was pretty in an unremarkable way but essentially rather inept in social situations. Trish was a natural unalterable innocent. She continually suffered from violent crushes on distant male figures with whom she had no hope of communicating for the simple reason that if one of her many heartthrobs had deigned to speak to her she would have swallowed her tongue and swooned dead away. She was sweet, however, and not nearly as harebrained as she appeared. Unfortunately, Gilly could not abide the girl, a fact of which she was fortunately unaware.

By the time Marta came in, huffy and glum as usual, Trish had driven poor Gilly to distraction. No one ever criticized Trish in Marta's hearing and got away with it though, and knowing this, Gilly shut his mouth and went into the kitchen to bring Laine to the table. She came in bearing a heaped bowl of yellow corn, with him at her heels like a wolfish hound ready to devour any morsel that might fall his way. Mary Judith hurried to bring the rest of the meal to the table, while Laine filled the glasses with cold tea. Trish asked anxiously if she could help and Marta and Gilly glared at each other over their plates.

Finally, with all in readiness, Mary Judith took her place between her daughter and Trish. All eyes went to the empty chair between Marta and Gilly. A place had been set, complete with glass filled to the brim with iced tea and a full complement of flatware. Mary Judith explained that they had a new boarder, but that he apparently had decided not to join them for dinner. She forestalled Trish's eager questions by suggesting that they pass the chicken before it got cold. Then, just as the laden platter began its journey, a door opened and closed and footsteps could be heard crossing the foyer. Mary Judith looked up expectantly, and a moment later her face lighted with a welcoming smile.

"Well, Mr. Tanner, we had about given you up. Won't you join us please?"

Trish gasped artlessly as the tall, dark-haired man walked to the vacant place and took his seat. Mary Judith bowed her head, covering a smile. One more unrequited love to add to Trish's ever-growing list. Quickly she started the platter on its way again and requested that Marta pass the baked squash.

Instantly the table was abuzz with movement and voice. Gilly asked for the creamed potatoes even as he drew the bowl to himself and scooped out his customary, overly large portion, which he drowned with thick brown gravy. This he followed with a mountain of small green peas, an obligatory serving of squash and two or three pieces of cooked carrot, all of which he dotted with margarine. He then launched a frontal assault on the bread basket and came up with three freshly baked whole wheat rolls, which he literally plastered with margarine. For the finale he added five heaping spoonfuls of sugar to his tea.

Mary Judith could not help noticing her new boarder's reactions to his companions. A mixture of concern and amused disgust on his face, Nolan watched the already obese man on his right heap his plate with unnecessary calories and dangerous cholesterol. He stared, seemingly fascinated until Gilly picked up his fork and dived in. At that point he turned away, carefully filling his own plate and darting small polite glances around the table.

Mary Judith was impressed by the demeanor of her newest boarder. Deeming him highly suitable, she smiled at everyone in general and looked about her for confirmation of her judgment. Trish, of course, was thoroughly smitten, and for once Marta appeared to approve. Gilly was much too intent upon his plate to give any notice one way or another, but the truly decisive reaction belonged to Laine, who was as obviously besotted as Trish with this tall, dark man. She stared at him with blatant adoration, and—to Mary Judith's everlasting surprise—he responded with warm solicitude. It was almost as if the two of them shared some intimate secret.

Mary Judith found this a bit disturbing, particularly as it became clear that this budding fondness was extended only to the daughter and not to her mother, as well. Indeed, Nolan Tanner seemed almost to despise her. His glances were increasingly pained, as if he found it difficult to look at her, and he seemed determined to avoid speaking to her directly.

At first, Mary Judith told herself that she was being foolish, and determined to play the part of the mistress of the house with gusto and feeling. She began a steady stream of bubbly conversation, some of it perfectly banal, and succumbed to the temptation to tease and laugh and flatter her companions. Within a half hour she was hating herself. Her words were forced and insipid, her manner obsequious to the point of desperation, and it had become painfully obvious that Nolan Tanner knew he was the source of her discomfiture.

He literally averted his eyes when she addressed him, while at other times she would turn suddenly to catch him staring at her with something very like pity in his dark-brown gaze. And still she could not stop herself. On and on she went, babbling about the weather and the state of the economy and—unbelievably—the prospects of life being found on other planets! Fortunately, only Marta and Tanner seemed aware of what was going on. Laine was too young to understand adult inanities, Gilly was simply too busy stuffing his face and Trish could see and hear only that which fed her own silly infatuation, none of which eased Mary Judith's embarrassment. When Nolan laid aside his fork, wiped his mouth with his napkin and came smoothly to his feet, she was as relieved as he to have the meal over with.

"That was a fine dinner, Mrs. Vickers," he said in a low rumbling voice. Her thank-you sounded twittering and high-pitched. "Thank *you*," he returned, and then as if he couldn't quite help himself he glanced at Laine. The girl beamed him a smile, which he acknowledged with a spare nod of his head and a quirk of his mouth. Then he quickly turned away and left the room.

Mary Judith wanted to die. Her head sagged forward and rested for a moment on the heel of her palm.

Then, thankfully, Gilly asked for yet another helping of creamed potatoes, and she forced her attention back to those at hand. It would be hours, however, before the mortification truly receded to a comfortable level and even then her cheeks would burn with color when she remembered that first appalling attempt to gain his favor and attention. She could call it nothing else for that was exactly what it had been—an attempt to impress him as much as he had impressed her. Later she'd be able to look at the incident with detachment and poise, but in the meantime there would be this cringing ache underlaid by a strange yawning emptiness. It was an ignominious beginning for love.

The needle and thread slid in and out of the fabric with the ease supplied by experienced fingers. Mary Judith paused periodically to check her progress. She was basting in a hem on a pretty little cotton dress. Her wardrobe had begun to look a bit ratty of late, and she had decided it needed updating. The blue flower-printed lawn was not the sort of fabric she usually chose, and it was rather late in the season for the full-skirted, ruffled and flounced frock on which she had decided, but lately she had begun to feel feminine and flirty again. It was not a welcome feeling. She found ample occasion to wish that it might simply go away, but then she'd catch a glimpse of a tall, dark, handsome man and it would flood her with the force of a tsunami.

She had spent much of the past two weeks being angry at herself and avoiding Nolan Tanner, but the attraction was too strong to permit her to hide from him indefinitely. Gradually she relaxed and resumed

her normal routine, fully aware that she would be
thrown into contact with him and secretly glad of it.
In actuality, however, she saw very little of him. He
had taken dinner with the group only three evenings
out of thirteen, choosing instead, according to the
identifiable odors, to eat canned chili and corned-beef
hash warmed on the hot plate in his room. He was
away during the daytime, of course, and kept to himself at night. He had said something about a free-lance
job when his drawing desk had been delivered, and she
supposed that accounted for his evening hours.

Still, the sounds of his footsteps in the foyer had
become almost eerily familiar, and at times she found
herself thinking of Mick and that hour of transition at
the end of the day when he would come home from
work and the evening would officially begin. She
hadn't thought of Mick so much in a long while, and
in a way it was very pleasant to remember how it had
been. But in another way it was disturbing that this
stranger could evoke those memories by simply walking across the floor of her house.

A change had begun to take place in Mary Judith
the day that Nolan Tanner had called to ask about the
room, and she didn't know why that should be so.
Moreover, she could see certain changes taking place
in her daughter, too, and that made her wary. Every
afternoon, Laine somehow managed to be in the foyer
when Nolan Tanner came home. Mary Judith didn't
like the feeling that she was spying on the two of them,
but she couldn't quite subdue the need to do so. She
told herself that it was only prudent. A mother's duty
was to protect her child, after all, and Laine did seem
unusually drawn to the man. So she would stand close
to the door to their private quarters and listen.

Sometimes he would walk by Laine with nothing more than a soft hello. But he would occasionally stop to chat, and at those times Laine was suddenly more animated and gay than at any other, and Mary Judith found herself in the awkward position of actually being jealous of the attentions her daughter both gave and received. She knew it was silly of her, and she knew also that Laine needed the attention of a mature adult male. It was for this reason that she forced herself to remain a not-so-innocent bystander.

The fact that she increasingly admired Nolan Tanner didn't help matters a bit. There were afternoons when he took more time with Laine than one could reasonably expect. Mary Judith would hear him come in, his feet dragging, and there would be Laine's little voice inquiring hopefully if he was in a hurry. He would laugh and the sound would rumble around the foyer and warm it with its rich depth. He'd sit down on a lower step with Laine at his side and inquire about her day.

"Well, muffin, how did it go today?" And the little one would gush information. She could spell any number of intriguing words, read better than anyone else in class and "how come Wednesday is pronounced Windsday?" On and on she would go. Somebody had pulled someone else's hair, and so-and-so actually had to go and speak to the principal, or they were making sheep out of cotton balls and pipe cleaners but hers only looked like cotton balls and pipe cleaners, so she was going to throw it away. To that he replied that he knew exactly how she felt. He hated it when things didn't turn out the way he meant them to.

At those moments when the two of them really seemed to be communicating, Mary Judith would listen and feel a strange sense of déjà vu and think at once of Mick. Then she would suddenly feel guilty, for that was not Mick sitting out there on the steps with their daughter. That was a kind stranger who happened to live in their house and was turning her life upside down with his aloof presence. She liked to think that Mick would have been equally patient and caring with Laine, but she couldn't help feeling that there was something special about this man, something more special than anything she had ever known, and then the ache would come again, the ache and the emptiness.

Then there were those couple of brief encounters that had nothing whatsoever to do with Laine. Once, Mary Judith had been working in the flower beds on either side of the front steps to the porch when she had suddenly felt as if she were being watched. She had turned her head to find him standing there, staring down at her as she knelt on the grass. Self-consciously she had reached out to touch a shrub with a waxy leaf.

"Er, as soon as the weather cools, we'll have both gardenias and roses," she explained. He had simply nodded, and his mouth twisted at one corner as if he would have liked to smile. "They're really magnificent," she bubbled on, "the fragrance is heavenly!"

He had started up the walk and climbed the steps to the porch, saying as he passed her, "I shall look forward to it." At the edge of the porch he had paused to look down at her with those dark, seemingly impenetrable eyes, and suddenly she felt...*happy*. She had said to herself then, *He thinks I'm pretty.* But the next moment she had denied the thought and a moment later she was frowning.

Another time, he had come home in the middle of the day. She had heard his footsteps in the foyer and for some inexplicable reason had opened her door and stepped out into the hall to greet him. This time his smile had been unrestrained, and he had come over with his key in his hand to lean against the wall and chat about nothing in particular. He had smiled a lot that day, and that was what she remembered of it now, that he had smiled at her, that he had seemed content, even eager, to be there with her doing nothing more than passing the time of day.

They were such common things, such mundane little episodes, why would they not leave her mind? What was it about him that wouldn't let her alone? Why should her life suddenly seem less than it had before?

The phone rang and Mary Judith put down her sewing to answer it. She walked through her small living room, and as she passed she straightened the crocheted doily on the old pedestal table where her grandmother's vase sat. She reached the telephone desk that had once belonged to her mother and sat down in the seat that curved out from the side of the drum, upon which the telephone rested. She lifted the receiver to her ear and greeted the caller in her husky, dulcet tone.

A man's voice said, "Is this where Nolan Tanner lives?" Mary Judith replied that it was, and the man at once launched into a disjointed explanation as to why he wanted to know. "I've been concerned... well, I suppose he's all right. He's been rather difficult to track down, but I guess I can understand that, how he's feeling, I mean, about the...difficulties he's been having. I just wanted to be certain that he's okay. He is okay, isn't he? Is there anything I can do?''

Mary Judith blinked at the telephone, uncertain what she should say. "I, er, Nolan is—just fine." There followed a strange silence, during which her brows crept together.

"I see," said the voice. "You're taking good care of him, are you?" Then came the sound of a deeply drawn breath. "Well, at least he had someone to go to. I'm glad of that. You must understand, I'm not sure I can approve of this living arrangement, but I'm grateful if you're helping him."

As the implications became clear, her mouth fell open, and she stared at the phone, shocked that anyone would think she was living with a man obviously not her husband. Yet there had been no mistaking his meaning. Before she could correct him, however, he rattled something about telling Nolan to call if he needed anything, thanked her for talking with him and hung up. Mary Judith dropped the receiver into its cradle and sat staring at it for a full minute. She had failed to get the man's name. He was obviously a friend of Nolan's; yet, strangely, he hadn't even asked to speak with the person he had called about! But none of that mattered to her as much as the fact that the man, whoever he was, actually believed she was living with—sleeping with—Nolan Tanner.

Another thought began to formulate in her head. She slowly stood. So, Nolan Tanner was the sort of man who went from one woman to the next without even bothering to cover his indiscretions. Otherwise, why would the man on the phone have jumped to the conclusion that Tanner was living with her? That was one conclusion she was going to have corrected as quickly as possible. And then she was going to have to rethink her opinion of this man. It was almost a relief to know something disparaging about him. It helped take the edge off her attraction to him. But it was disappointing, too.

She felt extremely foolish, all muddled up inside, like a schoolgirl suffering her first disillusionment. She walked across the room and took up the delicate lawn dress she had sewn for herself. Suddenly it seemed to have lost its appeal, and she quickly put it away. *Foolishness,* she told herself as she gathered up her sewing things, *pure foolishness.* She chewed her lip, wishing that she didn't have to speak to him about that call. Maybe she wouldn't. Maybe she'd just let it slide. Whoever that was would surely learn of his mistake as soon as he made personal contact with Nolan Tanner. Yes, she'd forget about it, forget about this infatuation with Nolan, too. She wasn't Trish, after all, or Laine. She was Mary Judith Vickers, a mature woman, a mother, a widow. She might as well face the fact that love only happens once in a person's life and she'd had her turn already. Even if she hadn't, love with a man like Nolan Tanner...well, it was simply out of the question. Out of the question.

Chapter Three

It was late when Nolan Tanner came home. Laine had waited in the entry hall until her mother called her in to set the table for dinner. She had, as was now the custom, laid him a place at the table, which he did not appear to want to fill. At some point Mary Judith had almost stopped expecting him and turned her mind to other matters. The evening passed pleasantly enough, and the child was in her usual state of good cheer when her mother tucked her into bed and heard her prayers.

Mary Judith, however, was not as calm as she appeared. She was troubled with vague dreads and unnamed excitements. She had decided that she wouldn't discuss the matter of the phone call with him, but as the minutes and hours passed, she found herself questioning that decision.

An ear cocked unwillingly for the sound of his coming, she sat through the evening news without really seeing the picture on the television screen or hearing the words of the commentator. Finally she switched off the set, checked on her peacefully sleeping daughter and slipped out into the foyer. She hesitated for a moment in front of his door, then turned and quickly walked out onto the veranda.

A yellow light burned on either side of the door, bathing the center of the porch in a delicate golden glow and casting the ends into shadow. Mary Judith walked to the east edge of the porch and paused outside of her own bedroom window. From there she could hear Laine if she cried out in her sleep. She settled down against the windowsill, one leg swinging free in the space between the edge of the porch and the boxy shrubs that grew beneath the eaves of the house.

The night was warm and lazy. Gleaming white moonlight painted broad strokes across the black canvas of the night. The trees stood in shaded relief, black against black dappled with diaphanous silver. Mary Judith felt herself growing still and wondered at the silent beauty around her. Soon a familiar peace crept over her, and she closed her eyes and allowed her head to loll back against her shoulders, her nostrils flaring as they filled with the clear, velvet air.

Life again seemed on an even keel, and she laughed to herself, wondering what on earth had possessed her to entertain thoughts of romantic involvement with Nolan Tanner. He wasn't her sort at all. Mick had been sweet and gentle and innocent, while Nolan Tanner was a man of the world, a sophisticate as out of place in her establishment as a butterfly in a beehive. Perhaps, she told herself thoughtfully, it wasn't Nolan at all. It was time. Perhaps it was simply time to realize that she wanted a man of her own, a husband, a partner, a friend. The days of magic and passion were long past for her. They had died with Mick. But maybe it was time to start thinking about dating again. There were men, after all, in the same boat as she, men who wanted a little convenience and mature companionship, average fellows who wanted average women.

She cocked her head to one side and opened her eyes, staring at the black roof of the porch. Nolan Tanner was no average fellow, that much was certain, but what was it about him that made him so different? Almost as if her thoughts were materializing, she became aware of the throbbing of an auto engine as it drew near behind a column of light, slowed to a stop at the curb at the end of the walk and evaporated into the silent darkness. Mary Judith got to her feet in time to see Nolan exit the expensive domestic sports car by the driver's door. He moved slowly but with sureness and purpose as he bent to retrieve several rolls of paper from behind the seat. He locked the door and closed it, then started up the walk with a smooth, long stride, the rolls tucked beneath his arm.

Mary Judith's heart began to pound in her chest as he drew near, the chaos descending upon her again. He reached the short flight of steps and climbed them, the soles of his shoes squeaking faintly against the painted treads. As he set foot upon the porch, Mary Judith suddenly shot forward out of the shadows as if propelled by an unseen hand. Startled, he drew up, halting there at the top step, slightly twisted, his broad shoulders squared. Mary Judith's fingers coiled about one another, trembled, separated, coiled again. Her thoughts were doing much the same.

"I, um, I need to speak with you." She winced, hardly able to believe that she'd launched into this thing after deciding positively not to. He nodded sharply, then seemed to relax by increments.

"Okay." He let the rolls of paper, blueprints, slide down into the cradle of his folded arm. "What's up?"

Mary Judith's hands itched and she rubbed them against the curved sides of her hips, the rough seams of her jeans scratching her palms. She bit her lips and leaned against the column that supported the porch roof.

"You had a call," she said at last. "I didn't get his name, but I expect you'll know who it was. He, um, spoke as if he'd had to track you down and asked how you were doing. Then he said you should call if you needed anything and, well..." She paused. The thing was difficult to say, especially to him. She swallowed the words, her eyes downcast and in shadow. Nolan Tanner fidgeted.

"Is that it? Well, don't concern yourself. I think I know who it was and I won't be needing his asssistance. I wouldn't call if I did, and he knows it. So forget about it. Doesn't matter." He stepped onto the porch and started past her, but she stopped him with a hand lightly placed at his elbow. She stared at her own hand as if uncertain it really belonged at the end of her arm, then stepped up and withdrew it, dropping it self-consciously at her side.

"There is something else," she rushed, "something that needs clearing up, a misunderstanding." She felt his gaze intensify and realized suddenly that the light fell fully upon his upturned face. She dropped her head, the sandy curls falling forward. They stayed there to frame her face when she looked up again, her position carefully renegotiated to put the light at her back. It filtered through her hair, making it a frothy halo of silvered half light that billowed cloudlike about a face softened by shadow. She could not know how compelling a picture she made or how that picture put the blood to throbbing at the base of his throat. He looked away.

"What misunderstanding is that, Mrs. Vickers?"

The formality of the title seemed ironic, even a bit ridiculous. She heard her laughter waft gently upon the night air and was surprised to find herself relaxing. "I think you could call me Mary Judith," she said, "considering the suppositions that have been made."

"Suppositions?"

She composed her face into an expression of serenity and subdued emotion. "The man who called," she said evenly, "assumed that the two of us are living together as...as a *couple*, if you take my meaning."

He did. The dark head came round smoothly, pointedly, and she knew that he was staring at her from the ovals of dark shadow that veiled his eyes. For a long moment he said nothing. Then his mouth curved slowly into a cryptic smile, and he lifted a hand to place a finger behind his ear.

"Ah. Well, that confirms it. I'm sure I know who called now. Only he would jump to such a conclusion. Just forget it. What he thinks doesn't matter."

Disappointment washed over her. What had she expected? She wasn't certain, but she had expected more than this casual acceptance, this unconcern. Her chin came up sharply. "It matters to me, Mr. Tanner."

Again, that cryptic smile. "*Mr. Tanner?* A moment ago we were on a first-name basis." Mary Judith felt a surge of unreasonable temper.

"How can you take this so lightly?" she demanded. "Perhaps your own reputation means nothing to you, but I thought you'd have more common decency than to allow an innocent person to be misjudged because of your...philandering!"

"Philan—" He broke off, a hint of amusement underlying his indignation. He laid a finger alongside his nose, his mouth quirking. "My, we are Victorian, aren't we?" he commented lightly and rocked back on his heels.

Mary Judith's mouth fell open. "Victorian! Well, I fail to see what's Victorian about protecting one's reputation! A woman in my position has to be very careful. I-I mean, I can't have people jumping to conclusions about things like this. After all, this is a boardinghouse, n-not a...bordello!"

"Ah. So it is." He compressed his mouth tightly, but it snaked upward at the edges, wriggling into a curvy grin. Mary Judith tossed her head.

"You aren't taking this seriously at all!" she charged.

"Oh, but I am," he assured her, his grin vanishing in a look of utter solemnity. "We can't allow people to get the wrong idea. The truth is what's important." He whacked a fist into a palm. "Why, one person spreading a falsehood can convince the whole world! First, complete strangers start to believe; then the neighbors get word; and finally, even those people closest to us have to wonder what's going on."

Mary Judith nodded agreeably, relieved that he understood. "That's exactly what I mean. One person jumps to the wrong conclusion and before you know it everybody else is doing the same thing." He nodded his head in hopeless disgust.

"Ah, and while we're talking about people jumping to the wrong conclusions," he said, his tone hardening, "let's talk about the running leap you just made, hm?"

Mary Judith blinked. "I, I don't quite understand what you mean." Nolan tossed his sketches into the lawn chair that sat in front of his bedroom window and brought his hands to his hips, his dark head inclining forward.

"Here you are lambasting me for something someone else has assumed while you've just leaped to a couple of pretty startling conclusions yourself! First, you accuse me of taking advantage of women. Second, you assume that I have or would live with any woman willing to share her bed! Well, those are a pair of far leaps, lady, and you missed the mark on both counts. For your information I have too much pride and too little time to go around taking advantage of females with more emotion than brains, and I haven't lived with a woman since my mother died when I was ten years old!

"Now, Miss High and Mighty, I suppose you'll find some reason to kick me out of here. Well, that's just fine with me. You say the word and I'm out of here—tonight!"

Mary Judith's face throbbed, but she didn't look away as her embarrassment urged her to do. She didn't look away because he was right and because there was no justification for her unfavorable judgment of him. She didn't look away because she was not ashamed to say she was sorry—and because he wasn't right about everything. She stood there and stared up at him with big, green, glittering eyes.

"I'm sorry, Nolan," she said quietly. "I was wrong."

Something very special happened then. The sternness and the aloofness in that handsome face just drained away, and suddenly those dark eyes warmed and flashed uncertainty. He stared at her, his head jerking to the side, his shoulders lifting in a shrug.

"Hey." He waved a hand dismissively and struck a rather self-conscious pose, one knee flexed, the other taking the bulk of his weight. He seemed terribly young in that moment, with the awkwardness of a teenager discovering for the first time what it is to communicate with the opposite sex. She wanted to reach out and take his hand and smile up into those dark, mysterious eyes and tell him to relax and be himself. "That's okay," he said, his manner self-conscious and careful.

"It's not okay," she protested gently. "I've offended you." She looked down at her hands and sucked in a hurried breath. "If you want to leave, I'll understand, of course."

"Oh, that." He lifted a hand to the back of his neck. "Yeah, well, I didn't exactly mean I wanted to leave. I just meant...well, no use hashing this over. Let's just forget about it, okay? It was all a big misunderstanding. I mean, these things happen."

"Yes," she agreed, "misunderstandings do happen." He nodded, and Mary Judith nodded, too, thinking that some misunderstandings were more damaging than others and wondering if she dared pursue that avenue of thought.

"Well, at least we cleared this one up," he commented, his dark head still bobbing.

"Yes," said Mary Judith. "We cleared up this one," she continued, putting a slight emphasis on "this." He shot her a pointed look, which she quickly feinted. "I, um, I ought to let you get inside." She turned quickly, but then his hand was suddenly there on her forearm and she froze as heat radiated from his grasp.

"Wait."

Slowly, very slowly, her heart pounding in her ears, she turned her head to stare at him. She meant to ask him what he wanted, but the words just couldn't seem to get from her brain to her mouth, so she stared at him, her green eyes glittering like emeralds in the golden light.

"I, um..." He stopped and cleared his throat. "I'll set the other straight. The call. I'll fix that."

The breath rushed out of her, and she was surprised to find that she had been holding it inside. Her knees felt watery, and her arm burned where his hand covered it. "Thank you," she said, dismayed to find her voice had gone husky and soft. She stiffened her spine, dismissed the trembling weakness in her limbs. "I appreciate that. I, I wouldn't ask you to do it, but...there's Laine to consider. I wouldn't want people saying...believing...things...for her sake."

"Um-mm." It sounded distracted, distant.

She looked up sharply, surprised to find him standing so near, looking down at her with those dark, mesmerizing eyes, as if trying to see inside her head. She felt the slightest tug on her arm, the gentlest urging, and almost against her will she found her body swaying toward him, her head slowly falling back against her shoulders. His free arm came up and closed about her waist, and she felt herself dragged forward and then felt the hardness of his chest as she met it. His hand left her arm and closed in the hair at the back of her head, his fist taking the weight of it as her strength melted away. The dark eyes delved into hers, and it was as if their gazes touched, as if they were joined by sight, bridged, connected. He seemed to be asking her something, to be demanding a reason for what was about to happen, and then it was as if he simply gave it up.

The dark lashes shuttered down, and at the same instant his hand splayed against the back of her head, and there was his mouth fitted against hers, just *there* at first, as if that were all he dared. Her own mouth trembled beneath his, as timid and uncertain as the arms that slowly moved upward and closed about his neck. And then suddenly she asked herself why. Wasn't this what she had wanted, what she had secretly hoped for, what she had ached for almost since the first moment she had met him? Whether it was right or wrong, she didn't know, only that it was what she wanted, what her body clamored for.

As if of their own volition, she felt her mouth soften beneath his, felt her arms grow languid and her hands possessive as they pressed against his shoulder and the back of his neck. His mouth widened in response, engulfed hers, plied it, searched it as a new landlord makes himself familiar with what is suddenly his. His arms tightened, and she pressed herself against him, allowing him every access, reveling in the abrupt demands of his need. His tongue shot into her mouth, scouring its high, velvety ceiling, tangling with her own, sliding along the sharp, clean edges of her teeth, then retreating, curling as if in invitation for hers to follow.

Suddenly the invitation was revoked and he jerked his head up. The dark eyes were wide with alarm, and Mary Judith's breath caught in her throat as she plumbed them for confirmation of the need she had felt in him, the desire. His hands held her face, his thumbs pulling the skin tight across her cheekbones.

"Damn!" he said, and there it was, the bright hot flame of passion burning deep within the brown tunnels of his eyes, behind the doubt, the anxiety, the brittle veneer of reluctance. "I didn't want this!" he growled. "Damn you, I didn't want this!" He sucked air through his teeth, and for a heart-stopping moment she thought he would push her away. But his head came down and his mouth claimed hers with a vengeance, a fierceness that left her no choice, no option at all except to give herself over to it and let him plunder as his need dictated. His hands slid down her body, cupping her hips and pressing her hard against his loins. For an instant she was frightened—and then she was his, simply and totally his, without the least will of her own, without even a thought of resistance. Her body had a new owner. She was just its inhabitant.

A car full of young people sped by and honked its horn, and it was like the gong of a clock signaling that time and reality had begun again. They jerked apart, simultaneously turning their heads toward the street. Mary Judith gasped, suddenly ashamed and uncertain. Nolan twisted away.

"Go inside!" he told her with anger in his voice. Anger! She bristled automatically, but when he repeated his command she quickly turned and hurried inside, stopping only when a trio of doors had been closed between them. There in her bedroom she undressed with shaking fingers and crawled beneath the covers, a million disjointed thoughts streaking through her head. She was shaking still when the exhaustion of confusion closed her eyes in sleep.

Nolan stood for a long moment, scowling at his bleary-eyed reflection in the mirror. He'd kissed her. He felt like kicking himself. What had he been thinking? He snorted derisively at that. That was just it. He *hadn't* been thinking, not at all. Even now, he couldn't quite think how it had happened. One moment he'd reached out with a hand, and then his arm had closed around her and suddenly there had been that luscious mouth turned up to him. He shuddered, seeing again the slackness of the full pink lips, the anticipation in the turn of her head, the green of her half-lidded eyes....

The passion swept through him again, that need, that fierce want of her. He knew that it was a feeling that would come to him over and over, at every unguarded moment, and he was sick with the knowledge of how he wanted her—and how that wanting jeopardized everything else he wanted and needed, all his plans and dreams.

If only he hadn't kissed her, felt that sweet yielding in her. No. It would not work, not with her. Not with Laine. Oh, yes, Laine was very much a part of it. She was proof that Mary Judith was the sort of woman who would demand it all: motherhood, wifedom and a license signed by the duly appointed representative of the tie-and-bind law. He wasn't ready for that. He simply wasn't a candidate. His own life was in such a mess. He had to straighten that out first.

He closed his eyes and bent over the sink to splash cold water on his face. First. What first? He was going to straighten his life out, period. He was going to concentrate on that and nothing else. He was going to work like a madman. And he was going to keep his distance from Laine and Mary Judith Vickers.

He thought briefly of talking this over with Mary Judith, of telling her exactly how and where he stood, but he saw himself sitting down with her, staring into that soft, lovely face with its glittering emerald eyes and its halo of tan curls. He saw Laine coming into the room and twining her little arm about his neck and looking up at him with that worshipful, copper-colored gaze. He saw himself cast in his father's role, the husband and father, working all the time while his wife slipped quietly away from him and his son clamored inwardly for some attention and recognition, some flash of understanding and acceptance. He saw himself being something he didn't want to be, something he despised, and he vowed never to let that happen. Never. Not even if it cost him everything, every hope, every plan, every possibility of getting it right again.

Mary Judith jerked awake. Instantly she shot upright in the chair and scanned the room unseeingly. Her eye snagged on the clock and she pushed her gaze back there and held it until it cleared. 3:20! She had slept away the afternoon. The last thing she remembered was coming in after taking Laine to school. She had been tired and had meant to sit quietly for a moment, and now the afternoon was gone and she hadn't yet gotten to the kitchen floor or thawed the roast for dinner or finished the blouse she was sewing for Laine.

Well, she could salvage something from the few minutes left to her. Laine would be home in little more than half an hour. That was enough time to run to the market and pick up a couple pounds of hamburger. They'd already had meat loaf once this week, so she'd have to do a goulash or something. No, Marta didn't like goulash. Maybe spaghetti, but that would make dinner late. Well then, she'd just fry up some hamburgers and serve them with chips and fresh vegetables. Laine would be pleased, especially if she globbed on the cheese and mayonnaise.

Mary Judith got up, straightened her slim pink cotton skirt and tucked the tail of her pink-and-white striped blouse into the waistband. She bent and quickly readjusted the strap on her sandal, then reached for her purse on the lamp table where she'd left it. It was at that precise moment that the telephone rang. The corners of her mouth tugged downward, but there was no rancor in her tone when she picked up the receiver and spoke into it.

"Hello."

"Hello, again."

She recognized the voice immediately, and the sound of it brought back that night, the night Nolan had kissed her, the night when the world had gone topsy-turvy and stayed that way. Her skin flushed with the memory of it. A single kiss in public view, only a kiss, nothing more, and yet it had not left her thoughts for more than a few minutes at a time since it had happened. That kiss had kept her awake nights, playing over and over again in her mind, the gorgeous face, the pliant mouth that fitted her own so well, the hands that molded and held and urged. She remembered it all: the musky male odor of him, the rasp of his beard against her chin and cheek, the feverish manipulations of his mouth, the warmth that swept through her, flashing white hot and robbing her of the strength of her limbs and will. She remembered it all, every second of it, and every empty second since then without him.

She shook herself, throwing off the curious nostalgia, the strange, uncommon melancholy.

"Um, this is Mary Judith Vickers," she said, remembering her manners. "To whom am I speaking?" There followed a brief moment of silence, a moment of uncertainty.

"This is Morgan Tanner," came the reply, and the saying of the familiar surname brought something else to her mind. It was the voice, but not only the voice. Something more. Something else. And then it hit her. Morgan Tanner. *The* Morgan Tanner. He sounded very like Nolan. So he was one of *those*, was he? She should have known. Merciful heavens, she should have known!

Pictures of Nolan flickered through her mind. Nolan in those expensive jeans, the shirts with the logos embroidered on the chest, the heavy gold watch, the sports car. Why hadn't she put all that together before? Of course he was one of *those* Tanners. He had money written all over him. So then what was he doing here? Why would *he* be living in a boardinghouse? She had the feeling the answer to that question was right in her hand. She pressed the receiver closer to her ear.

"Mr. Tanner, Nolan isn't home now."

"Ah. It's probably just as well, but I wonder if you mind speaking with me for a moment, Miss Vickers."

"It's *Mrs.* Vickers."

"Mrs...?" His surprise was audible, unmistakable.

So Nolan hadn't straightened out that misunderstanding at all. She probably shouldn't have expected him to under the circumstances.

"Forgive me, Mrs. Vickers, I'm afraid I misunderstood the other day when I called. I thought, I mean, I assumed that Nolan had...well, that an alliance of sorts had been formed between the two of you."

She cut him off. "Yes, Mr. Tanner, I know what you must have thought. But you were wrong, you see."

"Oh, certainly. I was completely off base. Frankly, though, when you answered the phone before, it did seem to add up. I couldn't imagine why he'd left Dallas for Denton. The friend who gave me this number only said that it was an 'unlikely' situation. I had no idea what he meant and he is something of a gossip, I admit; so naturally when you had answered the phone, well, I assumed that the unlikely situation of which my friend had spoken was, um, a romance, shall we say?" Mary Judith scowled at the phone.

"I'm Nolan's landlady," she said tartly. "He rents an efficiency apartment from me."

She heard a strange thump and then a screech, like a chair being shoved across a floor. "Oh my, I'm really embarrassed by all this. I'll have to find some way to let you know how sorry I am. Listen, you didn't...My son doesn't know about this, does he?" Mary Judith blinked at the wording of the sentence.

"Your son? Nolan is your son?"

"Why, yes. What did you think?"

"Well, I-I didn't know. I figured there was a connection, of course, but..." Morgan Tanner was Nolan's *father?* This was getting stranger and stranger. "Now, why," she muttered, "would a son of one of the wealthiest men in Dallas be living in a boarding-house?'' There followed a long silence, during which Mary Judith realized she had spoken aloud. ''Ah, I'm sorry. It's...it's really none of my business. I just meant...well...'' She looked around her, the phone held tight against her ear. This place must be a far cry from what he was used to.

''No, no, don't apologize. It's a long story, really, and an unfortunate one. Nolan's company has gone under. There were some improprieties, criminal activity, an ugly situation. Nolan's intent upon making restitution, of course, and I'm terribly proud of him for that. It was frightening, though. He could've gone to jail. I'm just thankful he's well out of it...''

Jail? Criminal activity? Mary Judith's brain went into a tailspin. Could Nolan have...No! She didn't believe it. On the other hand, what did she know about him, really? And if his own father could suggest...She closed her eyes, sick with the irrational feeling of betrayal, and interrupted him, speaking very quickly.

''Ah-h, Mr. Tanner, I don't think I should be listening to this. It's Nolan's business. Whatever he's done it's just none of my business, Mr. Tanner.''

He said something about misunderstanding, about the wrong ideas, but she didn't want to talk about that anymore. It suddenly made no difference to her what he had thought was going on between her and his son. Nothing, in fact, made much difference. She told him firmly that she had to go and then hung up. She sat for several moments with her hand still on the receiver and stared at the telephone.

She was a fool, she decided grimly, an absolute fool. The first man in years, the first man since Mick for whom she had felt any real attraction and he had to be some kind of—what? She couldn't quite make herself say it. She just couldn't say the word "criminal" in the same breath with the name "Nolan Tanner." She just couldn't.

But there was one thing she knew for certain now, one thing about which she could have no doubt and make no argument. Whatever else he was, Nolan Tanner was trouble, and from this moment on she was going to keep her distance. No more longing for him to turn up at her dinner table. No more listening for the sounds of his footsteps in the foyer. No more reliving that one silly kiss. No more wishing and hoping he would show some real interest in her. This foolish, insipid, juvenile infatuation was over, and she thanked her lucky stars that nothing had actually developed between them.

It was all in her head anyway, she told herself sternly, a figment of an overwrought imagination. She needed to get out more, to see her friends more often, to stop making such a big deal of such a tiny incident in her life. But there was that feeling of betrayal, that crazy notion that something very real and very important had been taken away from her. There was that yawning emptiness that seemed about to engulf her, that dull, throbbing ache in her heart.

She was a grown woman, a widow with a six-year-old daughter and a reasonably successful business she had built from next to nothing. She was strong and capable and self-sufficient, and she'd never been easy prey. These things weren't supposed to happen to her. It wasn't supposed to hurt like this. But there it was. Disappointment. Disillusionment as big as life itself, and not a darn thing she could do about it. Worse yet, she couldn't say why it had happened this way. She couldn't admit, even to herself, that the impossible had already started to happen. She was falling in love.

Chapter Four

She wasn't going to be judgmental. She had decided that right off. That term "criminal activity" could mean a number of things, and it wouldn't be fair for her to stick some ugly label on Nolan without knowing all the facts, none of which were her business. Besides, he couldn't have done anything really bad or they'd have sent him to jail, right? And his father had said something about him making restitution. That sounded like embezzlement or something, nothing violent or dangerous. Besides, everybody deserves a second chance. So, she'd decided that she wouldn't ask him to leave. She'd just let things stay as they were. He was obviously avoiding her, and she intended to help him do that. There was just one problem: how do you convince a six-year-old that some people aren't what they seem?

Mary Judith wondered about that as she stood quietly watching her determined young daughter. Laine sat on the steps, her chin balanced against her knuckles, her elbows against her knees, a woebegone look turning her smile upside down and dulling her tawny eyes. Her sneakers were untied and numerous tendrils of inky hair had escaped the band holding her ponytail, but none of that took away from the stubborn set of the jaw or the willful flare of small oval nostrils. All in all, she made a pitiful picture, and Mary Judith wanted to throttle Nolan Tanner for it. She sighed and crossed the foyer to stand at the foot of the stairs.

"Laine, honey." The child swiveled to the side, neither speaking nor looking up. Mary Judith bit her lip. *Better go easy. Remember she's just a kid. There's a lot she can't understand.* She bent forward and extended her wrist, exposing the face of her watch. "It's getting late. Time to be thinking about bed."

Laine's mouth tightened into a pucker. "Tomorrow's Saturday." She sounded like she had a mouth full of marbles. Mary Judith nodded.

"Yes, I know," she cajoled, "but growing girls need their rest."

"I'm not sleepy," was the flat reply.

Exasperated, Mary Judith ran her hand across her brow. Blast that Nolan Tanner! This was all his fault. Unthinkingly, she allowed that anger to spill over.

"Laine, I want you to stop this. You're being ridiculous. This isn't a relative we're talking about or even some school chum. He isn't an important person in your life, and you've got to stop pretending that he is!" The child stared at her with horror-filled eyes. In them, her mother could see a world thrown into confusion.

"But I like Nolan!" the child wailed. Mary Judith raised a hand to the bridge of her nose in frustration.

Of course, she liked him! And her feelings counted, but how did she make her understand that sometimes it was better *not* to like someone? She went down on one knee and wrapped her arms about her daughter's narrow shoulders.

"Laine, darling. I know that you like Nolan, but I'm afraid...I'm afraid..." Dared she do this, say this? It seemed so cruel, but she had to tell her something. She had to put a stop to this one-sided relationship. She took a deep breath. "Laine, I'm just afraid that Nolan doesn't really..."

"Doesn't really what?" The familiar voice sent chills up her spine. She jerked around, her mouth agape, the color draining from her cheeks.

"Nolan!" Laine sprang to her feet and raced down the stairs and across the floor to where he stood just inside the opened door. She threw herself at his knees, her arms going round his legs, her little head falling back upon her shoulders. "I missed you!"

Mary Judith wanted to cry. There was such heartfelt fondness in that child's voice, such honest emotion. To his credit, Nolan heard it, too. His hand went to the back of her head, and he looked down at her with a smile curling his lips.

"I've missed you, too," he said warmly, and the child returned his smile, so obviously content with this little attention that her mother felt a stab of resentment. As if privy to her feelings, Nolan looked up sharply and impaled her with a pointed, accusatory stare. She lifted her chin defensively. For a long moment they glared at each other, silently trading charges, then he tugged his gaze away and settled it gently upon Laine. Smiling, he disengaged himself, stooped and lifted her in his arms. The child laughed

with delight, and for several moments thereafter Nolan kept her giggling with teasing questions and comments. Then he said something quietly to her and she
nodded, reluctantly at first and then with more eagerness as he continued speaking. He put her down and
gave her shoulder a pat, and she glanced up with that
adoration shining in those big bright-as-new-pennies
eyes, then scurried away, announcing that she was
going to get ready for bed.

Mary Judith made as if to follow her daughter, but
Nolan stopped her with a direct look and a spare shake
of his head. She sank down onto the steps, her heart
pounding so violently she could hear it as if it were
right inside her ear. Nolan waited until Laine had dis-
appeared into the apartment before coming to stand
at the foot of the stairs. He turned to the side, angry
perhaps, obviously uneasy. Mary Judith looked away
from that honed, striking profile. If only he weren't so
blasted good looking, it would be so much easier to
deal with her feelings.

"I thought she would be in bed by now," he said,
and Mary Judith looked around in surprise.

"What do you mean, you thought she'd be in bed
by now?"

He dug his hands into his pockets and turned to
fully face her, his shoulders lifting in a shrug. "Just
what I said, I thought she'd be asleep."

She came to her feet. "Do you mean to tell me
you've been staying out late just so you wouldn't have
to see her?"

He held her gaze for a moment, then abruptly
looked away, his hands pushing through his hair. "I
thought it would be best," he began. "I never meant
for her to get so attached to me! I thought if I just kept

my distance she would kind of gradually forget I was around. I, I just—'' He broke off, the muscles in his jaws twitching with unspoken words. ''I don't want to see the kid get hurt, all right?'' He was practically shouting now, and made a concerted effort to lower his voice. ''Look, I really don't think it's a good idea for her to be so attached to me.''

''Well, neither do I!'' Mary Judith snapped. ''In fact, I think it's a terrible idea.''

''Fine!'' He flung out his arms, shouting again, but immediately regretted the outburst. He clenched his teeth and slanted a glance upward. ''Fine,'' he repeated quietly. ''At least we agree that it's best if she doesn't start counting on my being here all the time.''

She wanted to slap him. Her palm fairly itched with the desire to do it. Couldn't he see, the conceited monster, that it was too late for that? Wasn't it obvious in the way that child looked at him that she wanted to believe he was going to be around forever? It seemed to her then, irrationally perhaps, that he had led them on, each in her own way, made them think about him, made them care about him and then dashed their hopes and hearts like so much excess baggage to be discarded at his convenience. Nothing she could do was going to stop that little girl from being hurt, just as nothing would make her own disappointment less acute. And the crazy part was that she couldn't account for it. She didn't know why she'd felt so compelled to care about this man, why her child should be so instantaneously wrapped up in him.

''Oh, yes,'' she muttered, ''we certainly do agree!'' She pushed past him, unable to stand there and stare into those shimmering brown eyes one moment longer. She wanted simply to be away from him at that point, to know that her daughter was safely distant, but he stopped her. His hand closed around her wrist as she started forward and he turned her back sharply.

"You can't walk away from this," he insisted. "I want to know what you're going to do about it!"

She fought his grip, twisting and tugging until her arm was sore and burned from the friction. "It's none of your business," she declared, "how I choose to handle my own daughter. Don't worry, though, I'll see to it that she doesn't bother you again!"

"Oh, hell, Judith! It's not that. I'm not concerned for myself, it's her. She needs a solid male in her life, somebody she can depend on, somebody more than that fat toad Gilly! She needs the same kind of man you need, a man who can spend the proper time and attention..."

"How dare you!" She wrenched herself free and stepped back, anger bringing new strength and rashness. "How dare you make that kind of judgment! How would you know what I need, what my daughter needs? I'll tell you something, we don't need any man. Someday we may *want* a man, Nolan, but we don't *need* one, least of all an a-arrogant, s-self-centered—criminal!" That word fell like a first blow, wild and frantic and propelled less by harmful intent than confusion and pain. She knew immediately, even in the midst of raging anger, that it had been a mistake, a low, sorry hit. But there it was, done, and nothing to do now but defend herself.

He recoiled initially, a kind of stunned horror on his face, then he reacted just as she would have done, he lunged forward, charging in the face of assault and seized her. "What?" he roared, shaking her. "Are you calling *me*...?" He couldn't even say it, and that wild-

eyed glare told her it was a word best left unspoken
again by either of them, just as the hands that bit into
her upper arms told her how easily they could crush
her, how suddenly and quickly she would lose in any
real fight with him. That knowledge must have been
reflected plainly on her face, because all at once he no
longer seemed out of control. He was angry, yes, perhaps even hurt, but very firmly, very definitely in
control.

"My God, you believe it!" he said, and released her
with a little push that sent her stumbling backward
into the curled end of the banister. She grabbed it for
support, fear draining the color from her face, but a
different fear, the kind that makes one wonder how
much damage one has done, how much pain one has
inflicted. "Fine," he said in a grim voice. "Believe
anything you want. Tell the kid anything about me at
all, anything! Just stay away. You get that? The both
of you, just leave me alone." He turned and walked
out the way he had come in, leaving her there with
those words between them like a brick wall, solid, un-
breachable, final.

Laine was mad. He just didn't want to be friends,
her mother had said, and Laine had known without
having to be told that her mother was as disappointed
as she. It seemed cruel and stupid and mean to a six-
year-old, and she just couldn't figure it out. He ought
to have liked them, lots of people did. They were
pretty nice folks, she and her mom. At least she had
always thought they were.

She thought of all the times her mother had put up
with Gilly's bad manners and Marta's foul moods and
of how she listened so patiently when Trish twittered

on and on about the dumbest things, and that all seemed pretty good and pretty nice to Laine. As for herself, well, maybe she forgot to say thank you sometimes and maybe she did do some things that she shouldn't, but she was always sorry later when she remembered, realized that it was bad, and didn't that count for something? Didn't it just count that she wanted to be his friend? Well, apparently not, and that was what was so hard to understand. It just seemed to turn everything all upside down, and she wasn't sure what to think or how to behave anymore.

She was confused. Everybody was confused. Her mother. Nolan. The whole silly, upside-down world. The rest of it was plain old pride, the kind that smarts when somebody seems to say that you aren't good enough or swell enough, the kind that very often makes you do the opposite of what you know deep down that you should.

That was why she'd pitched a fit for the book, why she decided she was going to have it even after her mother had said no, even after Mary Judith had explained that it was old and fragile and had to be handled with great care by an adult. It seemed to Laine that she was being told she wasn't good enough for that book, that even though it was hers, given to her by her own grandmother, she just wasn't fit to handle it, and she was just naturally bound to prove otherwise.

She sat on the couch and looked up at the top shelf of the bookcase where the dark-red binding and those glittering gold edges stuck out like an invitation to hidden treasure. It was hers for the claiming, and with twenty long minutes to kill before time to leave for school and mother up to her elbows in dishwater, it seemed like the perfect opportunity. She got up and walked around the coffee table to stand before that massive collection of books, most of them old and musty but treasured nonetheless. She knew she wasn't supposed to climb on the shelves, but those neat ceiling-to-floor stacks, row after long row, looked so solid, so permanent.

She wasn't at all frightened, not even when she reached up with one hand and grasped the edge of the shelf just above her head and then lifted her foot from the floor. She wasn't the least bit afraid, not even a little, and it wasn't really hard. In fact, it was quite easy for a strong, brave girl like her. In moments, there was that rich red binding within her reach, and she pushed upward to get it, closed her hand on it, felt its weight slip over the edge and into her palm and then the room moved. That was what it felt like, the room teetering and swaying around her, and suddenly she knew she was going to fall and it was all going to come crashing down on top of her and she screamed with all the horror a six-year-old could feel.

"Laine!" Mary Judith pushed through the swinging kitchen door in time to see the massive bookcase as it rocked away from the wall, Laine clinging frantically to its uppermost shelf, her feet slipping clear of the lower one upon which she had been standing. Judith ran forward, her arms going out to catch the falling child, knocked down again by the hailstorm of books, bric-a-brac and chunks of plaster. She was screaming for Laine to let go, envisioning her tiny body crushed beneath the heavy wood cases and hardbound volumes, trying to protect herself from the avalanche, grasping blindly for some way to save them.

She heard the thump, heavier and yet strangely lighter than the others, and knew with staggering relief that Laine had jumped clear. Then the weight of the bookcase was upon her, jamming her hand against the side of her face, her head against her shoulder. She pushed with all her strength, turning to get both shoulders into it, her head pressed forward now at a more natural angle, her legs wobbly but still beneath her, and the weight of the bookcase crushing down, ready to smash and flatten everything else in its path. There was no way to get out, no time to dart forward or to the side without being trapped beneath it on the floor.

"Laine." The child stared like a frightened rabbit caught in a headlight's beam. "Hurry, honey! Get help!" For one panic-stricken moment the child seemed not to understand, and Mary Judith searched her mind frantically for a more definite order. Was she alone in the house? Gilly. Gilly would be here. He never got out of the house before ten. "Laine, get Gilly. Hurry. Go to his room!" The child sprang up and tore from the apartment with her ponytail flying.

Laine's heart beat faster than her feet, thumping so hard against her chest that she could feel it in her throat and the pit of her stomach. Unthinkingly, she passed Nolan's door and raced up the stairs. It had been days since she had seen him or wanted to, difficult, confusing days when she had misbehaved more often than usual. She was no longer certain when he came or went but just then she would have been glad to see him or anyone who could fix this awful mess she'd made. If only Gilly could do something.

She pounded on his door, heard him grousing, recognized the sounds he made when rolling reluctantly from his bed. He stuck his head out and listened with irritation at her half-coherent pleas. She saw that he hadn't really heard her. She was a child, almost sub-human, certainly less important than he and there-fore automatically discounted.

"I'll get my pants on," he grumbled and closed the door in her face. Laine stared, knowing he hadn't understood and that it was all her fault. She ran back down the stairs, screaming, and found herself in front of Nolan's door.

Nolan! He was the only one who could put every-thing right. It seemed clear as day. She began pound-ing, calling, begging, and suddenly he was there, shaking her and demanding to know what was wrong. She poured out a jumbled collection of half-sentences, but somehow he seemed to understand, and she loved him for that, adored him, worshiped him. Even when he pushed her aside and ran for the apartment, she loved him and she didn't care what he'd done or what he'd said or if he ever loved her back even a little bit. He was there and that somehow meant the crisis was over and everything would be okay.

She looked up, still sobbing and with the tears roll-ing down her cheeks, and she saw Gilly standing on the landing in his underwear with his pants in his hands and his funny, pale, skinny legs sticking out like toothpicks crammed in a marshmallow, and suddenly she felt sorry for him in a kind of cringing, unpleas-ant way, so she sniffed and in a quavering voice she said, "Nolan was here so it's all right." And it was. Somehow, it just was.

Judith watched him leap over things to get to her. "Okay, honey, hang on," he soothed. "Are you okay?" he asked anxiously. "Are you hurt?"

"I don't think so. My back hurts, but I think it's just the weight. Hurry."

She hadn't needed to say that. He had already sized up the bookcase, judged it to be roughly fifteen feet wide, nine or ten feet high, and decided the best way to get her free. He stooped to wedge his shoulder beneath its end. "I'm going to push up. It'll twist, but don't be frightened, just get out of the way."

"It'll fall!"

"You can get out."

"No! The furniture. Move it first."

He scanned the room quickly. "Can't, babe. This room's too crowded." He worked his way underneath and pushed. Judith heaved in relief as the weight shifted from her. "Get out!" he commanded, but she shook her head stubbornly. They were all the material possessions she had, all she could think of as hers and hers alone. They were all that was left of a family, her grandparents, her parents, even her husband. She had her memories of them, but Laine had only the things they'd left behind, and she wasn't going to see them smashed to bits, not now.

"We can do it together, Nolan. If you help me push we can do it!" As she spoke she worked her way to the opposite end, shoving, hoisting, feeling the bite of sharp wooden edges against her hands, the pull of muscles long ignored and recently abused. She had her back to him, but she could feel him holding up his end, so strong, so determined. Thank God it was him!

"You're one stubborn lady," he groaned, and then he yelled "Push!" and she knew he was with her. The bookcase sagged against their unmatched strength, twisted, bucked, then suddenly lurched back against the wall.

They stepped back with sighs of relief, then Nolan put his arm around her, squeezing the back of her neck. His hand was moist and trembling. "You okay?" she asked.

"*Me?* What about you?" His hand ran down her back and along her shoulder to her arm. "You okay?" She nodded, but even as she did so her knees buckled and she felt almost as if she were turning to liquid. He caught her against him, and she pressed her hands against his chest, steadying herself, feeling the safe, solid bulk of him.

"Nolan. Oh..."

"You're hurt!"

"No. No. Really." She looked up, shaking her head. "Just frightened, just..." That brown gaze traveled over her face, searching, assessing, as anxious as that of any friend, any lover. Dear heaven, he cared. Want to or not, he cared, as surely as those were his eyes spilling concern and worry, as definitely as those were his hands rising to cup her face.

"Me, too," he whispered and put his forehead against hers. She closed her eyes, so grateful, so supremely happy in that instant, so whole.

"Looks like you got it whipped."

They turned arm in arm—so natural that way—to find Gilly in the doorway, pulling a shirt over his head. He'd put on not just his pants, but his shoes and socks and now his shirt, as well. Laine was looking up at him with a mixture of dislike and pity on her face, her bottom lip stuck out, her big eyes full of liquid sheen. It had been minutes, only minutes, three or four at the most, but Mary Judith knew instinctively that if she had had to depend on Gilly she would be lying in a broken heap on the floor now, waiting helplessly while he dialed, fully dressed, for the paramedics or the fire department or whoever. She put him resolutely from mind, as one puts away an unpleasant memory, and a perfectly irrational thought popped into her head. She glanced at her watch.

"Laine honey, you're going to be late for school."

"I might as well take her," Gilly said. "I'm up and dressed." He said it as if he was the only one in the room who had had the good sense to put on clothes. "Got to get my wallet and keys."

Mary Judith fixed her attention on her daughter. Laine had flattened herself against the wall beside the door and was staring now at the floor, her face a mask of guilt and misery.

"Come here, honey." Reluctantly the child crept forward, edged past the books and debris, never once looking up until she reached her mother's knee. Mary Judith knelt and hugged her. "It's okay, honey. I know you didn't mean to make it fall. I shouldn't have taken the book from you and put it there, but it was a very dangerous thing you did. You could've been badly hurt, Laine, then what would mommy do without her precious girl?"

"I'm sorry." Her voice broke, but the tears were held bravely at bay. Nolan couldn't resist patting the inky head, smiling a comforting smile, giving her a little wink. She averted her eyes, silently pronouncing herself unworthy.

"It's okay," Judith said again. "We won't ever have to worry about this happening again, will we?" She tousled her hair playfully. "You were so brave! You went so quickly and got help. Now I know how good you can be in a crisis! We learned a lot today, didn't we?" Laine cocked her head noncomittally, but there was less of a shimmer in those big round eyes, less of a tremble to those pouty lips. "You feel up to school?" Mary Judith asked, and the child nodded resolutely, perhaps even eagerly. Nolan wondered if she wouldn't feel better once she had gotten away from the scene of the disaster.

"I'll help your mom clean up," he told her, and she rewarded him with a thankful glance. "And I'll fix that bookcase so it can't possibly come down again, okay?"

"Okay!" He laughed, and Laine threw out her arms, catching her mother and Nolan in an awkward embrace. Gilly was at the foot of the stairs now, calling her to hurry, as if he had planned to do something more with his time than sleep it away. Laine rolled her eyes and jerked a thumb, indicating the foyer. "I got *him* first," she informed them. "But he had to put on his *pants* before he could come." She looked up at Nolan, and those big amber eyes filled with tears. "Thank you, Nolan," she said, her bottom lip quivering fetchingly. "I'm so sorry!"

He flashed a glance at Mary Judith, saw a pleading look on that lovely face, switched his gaze back to Laine. "What are you sorry for now, pumpkin?"

"I don't know," the little voice quavered. "But I must've made you mad or something!"

"Oh no, baby, no." Judith watched him go down on his knees, take the child in his arms—such strong arms—and hold her tight against him. "What could you have to be sorry for?" he said, brushing tendrils of hair from her damp cheeks. "Why, you're just about the most special little girl in the world, Laine, the very best, very dearest little girl I ever knew." Her arms went around his neck.

"You mean it?"

He had a bit of trouble then. His mouth sort of jiggled around the edges and he seemed to blink more rapidly than was normal. "Yeah, sweetie. I sure do mean it."

"Oh, Nolan!" She squeezed him hard, and when he stood with her and walked toward the door, he was laughing and his voice was strong and reassuring.

"You go to school now," he was saying, "and when you get home I'll have that thing fixed so good you can climb on it all you want and it won't budge an inch—ever. I promise."

He put her down and she scampered away, as happy and content as the first day he'd seen her. Mary Judith called out to her to have a good day, and she called back that she would, and then Gilly ushered her out the door and they were alone again. Only it seemed like the first time, and there was an awkwardness left over by all the emotion that had been exercised that day. He pushed his hands through his hair and gazed around him at the walls.

"That's some kid, lady, some swell kid."

Judith sat on the floor. "Yes, I know," she returned quietly. He seemed to cast about for something to say, then he turned abruptly and threw out his hands, apology in his eyes, tugging at the corners of his mouth.

"Judith, listen, about the other day..."

She shook her head, interrupting. "Nolan, as far as I'm concerned, we acted that evening like a pair of pretty evenly matched jerks, but today...Today you saved us. You really saved us. Thank you."

He stood there with his mouth open for a moment, his palms turned up as if beseeching her forgiveness, then he slowly let them fall and cocked his head to the side endearingly.

"Hey, you're just lucky I already had my pants on," he said, not bothering to add that he'd fallen asleep in his clothes, too tired to even undress. He needn't have. Now that she'd had time to notice, it was obvious that was what he'd done, but she knew, pants or no pants, he'd have been there to help, and that counted more than anything else.

Mary Judith smiled. "Lucky me," she said, and oh, it was so true, so wonderfully true, that she said it again. "Lucky me." And this time, he smiled, too.

Chapter Five

She wanted to tell him that whatever he'd done or hadn't done in the past no longer mattered, if it ever had, but somehow she just couldn't make herself bring up the subject. She was afraid to discuss the matter of his alleged criminal activities for a couple of reasons. He'd been so angry when the subject had come up before that she feared broaching it now would only instigate another argument and she hadn't the emotional energy for that, not after the morning's excitement.

The second reason was more complex. What it amounted to was a genuine reluctance to know the truth. She had convinced herself that Nolan Tanner could not be guilty of any serious wrongdoing, and she bolstered that conviction by remembering something else his father had told her, that he was proud of Nolan for making restitution. To her that said Nolan was sorry for what he'd done and that the so-called crime hadn't been serious enough to warrant real punishment by the authorities. That assumption made it easier for her to accept all these feelings she had for him. It also conformed more readily with the image of the Nolan Tanner who was so gentle and patient with her daughter, the Nolan Tanner who had come to her rescue this morning, the one who had kissed her that night on the porch and invaded her private thoughts for so long now. If the "real" Nolan Tanner was something less than the man she sensed him to be, she wasn't at all certain she wanted to know about it.

Why should she, after all? It wasn't as if she were contemplating marrying the man. Heavens, the very notion was absurd. They hardly knew each other. There could be nothing more than friendship in the cards for them, if even that, and then only in a temporary fashion as he'd made it plain that he wouldn't be around long. That was one fact she would do well to keep in mind.

Meanwhile he had been here when they needed him, and for that she was grateful. It would be silly, she decided, and ungrateful to bring up a subject that would undoubtedly cause him pain and trouble. So she kept her mouth shut, and the morning, in spite of its beginnings, turned out to be a splendid one.

Shortly after Laine left for school, Nolan went back to his room to shower and change while Mary Judith fixed him a light breakfast. She sat at the table and had a cup of coffee while he downed toasted English muffins and a grapefruit broiled with a topping made of margarine, rolled oats, and brown sugar. They made small talk, laughed too readily and pretended to be at ease with each other; and yet he seemed as willing to stay and keep his promise to Laine as Mary Judith was to have him do so.

After breakfast Nolan made a detailed inspection of what he jokingly called "the crash site," then made a list on the back of a business card of a few items necessary for repairs.

"I don't suppose you've got any plaster lying around here, do you? Or bedding tape or wall cloth, or maybe a good strong two-by-four by any chance?" Mary Judith shook her head no to each item. He laughed and tucked the list into his shirt pocket. "I didn't think so. Well, looks like I'll be making a trip to the lumberyard. I'm pretty sure I've got everything else I'll need in the trunk of my car. Ah, everything except a ladder."

"A ladder I've got," she said. "In the garage out back."

"Okay. That's that. Guess I'll be going then."

"What about money?"

He looked up, his brows arched in an effort to look innocent. "What about it?"

"You'll be needing some to buy all that stuff."

He shrugged. "Oh, don't worry about that. I've got an account with the local supplier. I'll just add this to it, and we can decide what to do about it later."

Mary Judith frowned. "I'm not sure I approve of that. Why don't you just let me give you some cash now? That way we won't have to worry about settling up later."

He smiled faintly and took her hands in his. "I'm not worried, not any longer." He glanced over his shoulder at the warped and splintered bookcase, and she felt him shudder. "You could've been killed," he said softly, "both of you."

"I know," she replied, "but you were here." His gaze snapped around, focused sharply on her face, held there for a long time. She could see the confusion in those dark-chocolate eyes, the same kind of confusion she so often felt herself these days, but there was something else, too, something that made her breath catch and set her heart to hammering eagerly.

"There's a lot to do," he said, dropping her hands. "I'll be back." She nodded and backed away.

"Meanwhile I'll clear out some of this mess, give you some room to work. Okay?"

"Sure." He seemed to draw into himself, and then he was leaving, stepping with long uneven strides over the heaps of books and bric-a-brac littering the floor.

"Nolan?" He halted, half turned. She laced her fingers together, suddenly feeling awkward and shy. "I just wanted to say...how glad I am that you came here. Laine and I, we want you to be our friend."

He looked as awkward and self-conscious as she felt, and she immediately wished she could take it back, just wipe the words right off the slate. Then he took in a deep breath, lifted his head high and met her openly. "You're a special woman, Judith," he told her evenly. "And if things were different with me...what I mean is that if I could see my way clear to—" He broke off and shook his head. "There's really no point going into it."

She wanted to ask why, wanted him to tell her what stood in the way, what kept them from doing what seemed most natural, from falling in love. But she feared it was all part of that thing she didn't want to know, and so she merely nodded as if she understood and he went out, closing the door on all the questions and on all the possibilities—or the impossibilities. That was the hard part, accepting the limitations, but it wasn't the first time life had imposed conditions on her, and she had always survived before.

When he returned with his supplies, she had everything ready for him. The books had been haphazardly stacked out of way, and she had shoved the furniture back as much as possible and swept the carpet free of glass. He brought the ladder from the garage and went right to work, stopping only long enough to wolf down a monstrous sandwich for lunch. Mary Judith made herself as useful as possible, fetching tools and mixing plaster. Soon the room began to take shape again.

The two-by-four was inserted into the wall horizontally as a brace and the bookcase was attached to it. The holes in the wallboard were patched and drying. Meanwhile he filled and sanded the splintered edges of several shelves and restained them, carefully blending the old with the new until the damage became invisible. By the time he had finished this task, the patches on the wall had dried and were ready to be textured. This time the drying would take overnight. The painting would have to wait until the next day.

Laine came home at three and found them kneeling together on the carpet, their hair full of sawdust, their faces smudged with white plaster. She was delighted to see that they were still at it, and after a bowl of peanut butter mixed with honey, she was right in there with them, laughing and talking and generally astonishing them with her quick wit and droll sense of humor while she stacked book after book, some four hundred of them, the accumulations of three generations of a family.

By six the books were all stacked in order, the furniture had been moved back into place, the figurines and pieces of glass that could be salvaged had been—a few sentimental tears were shed over the others—and the carpet had been thoroughly vacuumed. The books couldn't go onto the shelves until the next evening, but in the meanwhile it was mealtime again.

That brought Gilly in. He was a man who thought with his stomach, and it had never occurred to him that he might have to find his dinner elsewhere that evening just because of a little thing like near total devastation. He wrinkled his nose at the mingled smell of rubbing compounds and new plaster, groused about the inconvenience and proceeded to upbraid Laine for having caused the whole mess. Apparently it was a continuation of a speech delivered on the way to school that morning. Laine looked contrite and wounded, and Mary Judith was incensed, but before she could so much as open her mouth, Nolan had already leaped to the child's defense.

"Lay off the kid, Gilly. She didn't do anything every kid doesn't do at some time or other, and I won't have you making her feel guilty about it. If that bookcase had been anchored properly in the first place it never would've happened. But more to the point, you just don't go taking it on yourself to lecture her. She's not yours, you know."

Laine stepped close to Nolan's side and wrapped her arm around his leg. She gazed up at him with eyes that clearly said, "My hero!" Gilly noticed and stuck out his big belly in indignation.

"Well, she's not your kid, either! Come to think of it, what makes you think you've got more say-so around here than I do? I've been here a lot longer than you have, and I'll be here when you're long gone."

"You're out of place, both of you," Mary Judith put in sternly. The quietness of her tone implied an authority far outweighing any other, and she exercised it. "When it comes to the final say-so around here, it's mine, and so is Laine. So I'll thank you both to keep your comments to yourself." Nolan lifted a hand as if in surrender, then let it fall to the back of Laine's head. Gilly didn't take the censure quite as complacently. His face pulsated a brilliant red beneath his mousy-brown, unkempt hair, but he said nothing more.

Trish and Marta showed up just then and suggested they send out for pizza. Gilly ordered a submarine sandwich on the side and went upstairs to await the arrival of food without donating so much as a penny toward its purchase. Trish, who was her usual flighty self, was too busy batting her eyelashes at Nolan to be of much service, but Marta took the situation in hand, organized the food order and telephoned it in. Then, with more than her normal amount of poise and magnanimity, she quickly maneuvered Trish out of the apartment and volunteered to pick up the pizza.

Mary Judith readily accepted. "That would be great, Marta. Thanks."

Nolan tossed her his keys. "Here," he offered casually, "take my car."

The girl stared first at the keys in her hand and then at Nolan with a kind of wonderment. "You certain?" she asked. He shrugged unconcernedly.

"Sure. Why not?"

Marta narrowed her eyes, testing him. "That's an expensive, high-powered machine. How do you know you can trust me with it?"

He chuckled. "I just know. Now get out of here, will you? I'm starved."

Marta tossed the keys in the air and caught them. "Pizza coming up," she said, and left them with a smile on her usually solemn face.

"That was a sweet thing to do," Mary Judith told him.

Again he shrugged, explaining, "I know what it's like not to be valued by anyone. Marta strikes me as that kind of person, and it's a shame because she's got a brain behind that sour face, which is more than I can say for Miss Flirtation and the Walking Stomach."

Laine looked rather puzzled, but Mary Judith sputtered laughter. "No, wait," she said, pressing her fingertips to her mouth. "That's not fair."

He was grinning at her. "Why not?"

"Because it's the same way with Gilly and Trish," she asserted. He slanted her a doubtful glance. "No, I mean it. Think about it. Who really cares about poor Trish?"

"Marta for one," he observed. Mary Judith cocked a brow in capitulation.

"Hm, that's true."

"But Trish doesn't seem to particularly value Marta's friendship. She just accepts it as some mundane fact of life, like breathing." He shook his head. "I doubt Trish will ever realize what a friend and supporter she has in Marta until she loses her, and even then she'll probably be too busy mooning over some jerk who doesn't know she's alive."

"And Gilly? What's your objective opinion of him, doctor?"

He pulled in a cautionary breath. "Ah, I have none, not an objective one that is."

Mary Judith folded her arms and smiled smugly. "Just as I expected." She wrinkled her nose. "He isn't very likable, is he?"

Nolan tapped her on the end of that very pretty nose. "No, he isn't, but that doesn't keep you from caring about him, does it?" His voice had gone strangely soft at the end, and it sent a warm glow through her.

"I care about all my friends," she said, her gaze steady and strong. Her meaning did not escape him. He reached out and laid a palm on her cheek, and it was as if some invisible magnetic force were drawing them together, toward an ultimate, inexplicable joining. His gaze seemed to focus on her mouth, and the memories of a kiss shared in the golden glow of a summer night flooded over her in stunning, sensuous detail. And then something—someone—bumped against her, and she looked down at the watchful face of her daughter.

Nolan dropped his hand and rested it on Laine's narrow shoulder. There were splotches of color high on his cheeks, but his manner was smooth and gentle.

"It's good to have friends," he said, massaging that delicate shoulder. "Very good." Laine reached up and hugged him with her arms about his waist. He smiled down at her, then up at her mother. It was a tender, melancholy thing, that smile, and it said all there was to say about the way things were with them—and the way they simply could not be.

He left them at about seven, saying he had work to do, and she couldn't help urging him to take it easy. He'd already worked a full day, after all, and needed his rest like everyone else. He just smiled and said not to worry, he wouldn't be long, and then he slipped out the door, leaving her wondering if he meant to come back. She hoped he would, and after putting Laine to bed she bathed and changed clothes and actually sat around anticipating his return. Then, just when she had convinced herself she was being foolish and was about to opt for television, a knock came at her door, and she jumped up to answer it.

She should have known at once who it was standing outside her door, but because she had expected to find Nolan there, she was a bit too disappointed to really look at this person until he stuck out a hand rimmed by a cool gray cuff and a silver cuff link fashioned to look like a large square button. It was something about the hand itself that first hit a chord with her. Something about the long tapering fingers with the oval nails and the slender knuckles seemed extremely familiar, and then she thought of Nolan's hand as it had gently cupped the back of her daughter's head or gripped the metal shank of a hammer, and she looked up into dark-brown eyes and a face that was a leaner, older version of one she had seen less than an hour earlier in this very place.

"I'm Morgan Tanner," he said, and she reached up mechanically to take his hand, marveling at the face behind the dark craggy brows and the thick, distinguished mustache. It was the mustache, in combination with the wide gray shock of hair that fell across his forehead that had thrown her. With only the thicker brows and the threads of silver at the temples, he could have passed at first glance for his son. "I'm sorry to bother you," he said, and this time she recognized the deep, rather raspy voice as the one she had heard on the telephone.

"Oh." She realized suddenly that he had stopped shaking her hand and she pulled it away. "Mr. Tanner, h-how nice to meet you. I'm..."

"Mrs. Vickers," he finished for her. "And just as lovely as your voice. I'm delighted." He bowed slightly from the waist, the broad shoulders beneath the slate-gray coat tipping forward. He was thinner than his son, taller perhaps, and less robust, but in good shape. She wondered how old he was. Fifty? Sixty? The face seemed ageless. Only the teeth, which were slightly yellowed, and the graying hair showed signs of aging. He folded his hands and let them drop in a gesture bespeaking patience.

"Would you like to come inside?" she asked rather abruptly, but he shook his head.

"No, no. I was just looking for my son." He waved a hand absently, explaining. "The front door was open. I knocked but no one came, so I figured I would ask around. I hope that's all right."

"Of course. I don't usually lock up until ten o'clock, and then the tenants have their own keys if they come in late. We're pretty casual about that sort of thing."

"Ah. Well, if you'll just point me in the direction of my son's door..."

She glanced at the door across the foyer and frowned. "Yes, that would be the one directly behind you, but, um, he's not in at the moment."

A look of disappointment wrinkled his brow. "I see. Do you by chance know when to expect him?" She shook her head.

"No, I'm afraid not, but he did say that he wouldn't be long and that was, oh—" she glanced at her watch

"—nearly an hour ago." He nodded gravely and squared his shoulders.

"In that case I will come in for a spell, if it's not inconvenient."

Already she was wishing she could withdraw the invitation. He seemed like a perfectly nice man, but she couldn't help remembering that he had already complicated her life in a couple of ways. But it was even more than that which made her feel uncomfortable about allowing this man into her living room. It was a feeling that his presence would somehow bring about a change in her life, the strange notion that he was the key to a door she wasn't certain she dared to unlock. Why she should feel that way she didn't quite know; not that it mattered, since she had made the invitation, and now had no choice except to follow through with it.

She let him in and saw to it that he was comfortably installed upon her couch before apologizing for the cluttered appearance of the room.

"We had an accident this morning." She briefly explained, adding that Nolan had quite literally rescued the day. "I don't know what I'd have done without his help. It's sometimes difficult to find the right kind of assistance in a situation like that, especially for a woman in my position."

"Your position?" The question came back at her in very casual tones, but she suddenly felt awkward about answering it.

"I'm a widow," she replied quickly, hoping he would not perceive the slight hesitation and read anything significant into it.

"Oh. My condolences."

The reaction seemed completely natural, quite suave. She inclined her head.

"It was some time ago. Laine and I—um, that's my daughter—we've adjusted quite well, I think."

They chatted politely about the six-year-old sleeping in another room, but the list of casual topics on the subject soon exhausted itself, and Mary Judith turned the conversation back to Nolan and the morning's events. Morgan Tanner surveyed the repairs and nodded appreciatively.

"Looks as if he's done an excellent job," he remarked in a strong, clear voice. "But then he always was good at this sort of thing. He used to work for me summers when he was a teenager. The men always said he had a gift for building things, and he's certainly proved them right, every last one of them, and will again, unless I miss my guess."

He seemed very proud, and that softened her reticence somewhat, but she kept remembering Nolan's reluctance to even speak with his father on the telephone. That reluctance just didn't fit with the image she was forming of the man who sat before her now, and despite her qualms she couldn't quite suppress her curiosity. She picked at a tiny thread trying to escape a seam in the cotton slacks she wore and schooled her voice in a conversational tone.

"Nolan must have forgotten you were coming," she said. And then with a rather pointed glance, she added, "That doesn't seem like him, though."

A guilty look flashed across Morgan Tanner's face. A hand drifted up to tug at the knot of a charcoal silk tie. "Well, actually..." He shifted positions. Again his fingers lightly stroked the Windsor knot at his throat. "He didn't know I was coming," he explained reluctantly. "I had this sudden impulse over dinner, you see. So about an hour ago I hopped into the car, and here I am." He spread his hands, but the carefree gesture seemed out of place with the tightness about his mouth and the gathering brows. It was none of her business, and her best judgment counseled caution, but she decided to press him on the subject anyway.

"Nolan was just going out then," she observed. "Pity you didn't call first. Perhaps he could have saved you this wait."

He nodded sheepishly and crossed his long slender leg over his knee, displaying huge feet shod in expensive gray Italian leather. Then his face puckered in a grimace.

"Actually, Mrs. Vickers," he confided, fingering the crease in his pants leg, "it wouldn't have helped. On the contrary, calling ahead would have guaranteed my son's absence." He winced, as if the admission were physically painful to him. "Nolan and I are not on very good terms. I don't suppose we ever have been. And I doubt very much that he would have consented to see me had I called ahead."

Mary Judith looked down at her hands, sorry she had pressed the matter. "I see. Well, that explains it then."

"What is that, Mrs. Vickers?"

He leaned forward, seemingly anxious to discuss his son with her. Mary Judith warred with herself. She felt both compelled by and wary of the idea of discussing Nolan with anyone, let alone his father. She was keenly aware that she had no right to pry into his private affairs; and yet he so intrigued her and there was such mystery about him that she couldn't help wanting to know more. Perhaps this was what she feared, this weakness within herself, this inability to resist anything that had to do with Nolan Tanner. She remembered an old adage about looking before leaping, but leaped anyway.

She told Morgan about Nolan's reluctance to confront him on the assumption he had made about their living arrangements, about his promise to correct the situation and about his obvious failure to do so. From that point the conversation became increasingly personal, so much so that she found herself recoiling, only half listening as this wealthy, well-known stranger talked candidly of his estrangement with his son. It was not a particularly uncommon story: a rather undemonstrative man who had never become fully comfortable with his own emotions suddenly finds himself widowed with an adolescent son to raise, and not the least notion how to go about it.

By his own admission, he did everything wrong. He hid his grief and expected his son to do the same because that's the way it was with men: they didn't hurt; they didn't cry; they didn't talk about the things that tore at their insides. They were tough. When Nolan naturally reacted with confusion and rebellion, his father got tougher yet. It became an adversarial relationship. By Nolan's twentieth year they were at each other's throats constantly. When Nolan graduated from college he rejected his father's seemingly perfunctory offer of a job within the family building business and struck out on his own.

"He did quite well for himself," Morgan conceded, "and at a time when the market was narrowing. He picked up a couple of experienced partners, garnered some choice projects, secured excellent financial backing. Within six years, Tanner, Weedn and

Bonds was an economic force to be reckoned with. They were one of the big boys on the block. Unfortunately, a good portion of the business community had always believed that I was the power behind the operation. It wasn't so, of course, but some mutual contact was always running to me with reports and questions about Nolan's dealings. It did no good for me to say that I was merely an observer. No one believed it. And that was a terribly bitter pill for Nolan to swallow. He has his pride, after all, Tanner pride.''

Mary Judith had seen that stiff-necked pride of his firsthand the night they had argued. He'd walked off without even making a defense for himself, choosing to let her believe whatever she wanted rather than justify any past action. Oh, yes. He certainly had his pride, and she suspected it was a breed apart, more fierce than any she'd ever before encountered. She wondered just how far he would go to get out from his father's shadow, to stand in the spotlight alone.

"I suppose that was what was behind his trouble with the law," she muttered.

Her head jerked up in surprise as her guest exclaimed, "Lord, no!" He was suddenly on the edge of his seat, his spine stiffened, those dark eyes flashing outrage. "Nolan had no trouble with the law! It was those two partners of his. They were the culprits. By the time he found out what they were up to they'd siphoned off hundreds of thousands of dollars. Nolan's only mistake was in trusting them and in his agreement to the division of the labor. He was in charge of all actual design and building, while Bonds handled the financing and Weedn the corporate books. Weedn had an excuse for everything—every dissatisfied subcontractor, every outraged investor.

Most of their doings went completely undetected until the end when the cash flow was reduced to nothing." He looked down at his hands, so like Nolan's, and squeezed them into tight fists. "I was the one who finally caught on to them. I was the one who got all the scuttlebutt. I've had years more experience than Nolan in every phase of the business, so I was the one to finally put it together."

"And when you went to him with the information, that was just one more insult to that gargantuan pride of his," she surmised. He sat forward and, with elbows on knees, pushed his hands through his hair, then nodded gravely.

"Yes, that's about it." He sat up, looking suddenly much older, and concluded the story. "Weedn and Bonds went to jail. They tried to implicate Nolan to cloud the issue as much as possible and save their stinking hides, but it was only a matter of days before the whole thing was out in the open. They made plea bargains and went quietly to jail, leaving my son to face the mess they'd made. The police did manage to recover some of the missing funds, and Nolan used that to satisfy as many of his creditors as possible. There were some insurance benefits, but it wasn't nearly enough." He looked over at her, a kind of wonder on his face and a dark liquid sheen in his eyes. "Do you know that boy sold very nearly everything he owned and then took out a personal loan to pay back all the people who were swindled. The lawyers told him just to declare bankruptcy and let it be, but he wouldn't do it, not my boy, not my son."

Mary Judith sat and stared at him with big sad eyes. He wore that fatherly pride like a great royal mantle, and it crushed her to think that Nolan couldn't see it, didn't know how very much he was loved and admired. Worse than that, though, was the knowledge that she had so sorely misjudged him, so completely and unfairly allowed herself to believe he was a criminal, when in fact he was the most honest, honorable man imaginable. She was sick about it, sick at heart, and she didn't know how very much she looked like a forlorn little waif sitting there with her big green eyes shining soulfully and a halo of soft curls wreathing her head.

Her gaze wandered to the bookcase standing snugly against the wall with its big chalky patches of new plaster. He had done that for her and Laine, knowing all the while that she believed he had committed some heinous crime. How on earth could she make that up to him? How could she possibly balance the scales now? She wanted to cry. She just wanted to cry. It was then the clock over the mantel began to chime the hour and Morgan Tanner came smoothly to his feet.

"Good heavens, it's ten o'clock. I can't believe I've stayed so long. I'm so sorry I've imposed, Mrs. Vickers, and it's really all your fault." He charmed her with a smile. "You're such lovely company, so very easy to talk to. I guess that's what I needed, someone to listen to me." He took her hand and bowed low over it, a very gallant, very moving gesture that triggered a kind of instantaneous fondness in her. She smiled and gently patted his shoulder, as if he were a child with a scraped knee. He straightened suddenly and looked down at her, his dark gaze wandering over her face in much the same way that his son's had often done.

"May I ask you a personal question, Mrs. Vickers?"

"My name is Mary Judith," she said by way of consent. "I prefer people who ask me personal questions to call me by my given name." His smile broadened.

"Judith," he began, instantly christening her with the very name Nolan had chosen for her, "how long have you been in love with my son?"

She drew back, the muscles of her face tensing, her face pale, her eyes wide and wild, like those of a frightened animal. She looked away, words of denial balled on her tongue. But no matter how hard she tried they simply wouldn't roll out of her mouth. They seemed stuck there, all jumbled and twisted, until she finally swallowed them, tasting the soured pride from which they were made. She lifted a hand to her mouth and shook her head, fighting the tears that threatened to well in her eyes.

"I don't think he's seen it yet," she said in a hushed voice. Then with her shoulders squared, her chin aloft, she added, "You're very perceptive for a man out of touch with his own emotions."

He shook his head. "I'm not that man anymore, Judith, and that's what I want my son to see, that I'm not the father he learned to hate. I want my son to know that I love him." She nodded and didn't look up again, a humbling wetness gathering behind her eyelids. He crooked a finger beneath her chin, whispering, "Love should not be kept a secret, dear lady. Take it from one who learned that lesson too late, I fear."

She lifted her gaze then, let it say all that was in her heart, then stated it clearly so that there could be no doubt. "And what if it isn't returned? What if it's rejected?"

His eyes clouded and he shook his head sorrowfully. "I can't answer that. But I know this, Judith—" his finger uncurled beneath her chin, followed the line of her jaw with a strong, bold stroke imparting courage, confidence "—whatever the consequences, whatever the odds, love has to try. Remember that—for Nolan's sake, for your own—love has to try!"

Chapter Six

She had decided before Morgan Tanner had even gone that he was right, and she knew exactly what she had to do. Good and healthy feelings had sprouted between her and Nolan at the very beginning, and she was not willing to let them die now. They deserved a chance to grow, and she couldn't see a single reason why they shouldn't have it, not one.

Laine was sleeping quietly when she checked on her, and she stood by her daughter's bed for a moment, thinking how long the two of them had been alone without a father and husband and how it had ceased to matter in the years since Mick's death—until now, until Nolan Tanner.

Quickly exiting from the bedroom, she slipped through the living room and into the kitchen, where she kept a set of keys hanging on a peg at the end of the cabinet. She closed her hand around them, lifting them from the peg, and went out. She left her apart-

Slip away for awhile...
Let Silhouette Romance draw you into a love-filled world of fascinating men and women... **Take 4 novels PLUS a MYSTERY GIFT FREE!**

Silhouette ❤ *Romance*®

Silhouette Books, 120 Brighton Rd., P.O. Box 5084, Clifton, NJ 07015-9956

YES! Please send me 4 Silhouette novels FREE and without obligation PLUS my Mystery Gift...

Unless you hear from me after I receive my 4 FREE books, please send me 6 new Silhouette Romance novels for a free 15-day examination each month as soon as they are published. I understand that you will bill me a total of just $11.70, with no additional charges of any kind. There is no minimum number of books that I must buy, and I can cancel at any time. The first 4 books and Mystery Gift are mine to keep.

NAME   (please print)

ADDRESS

CITY   STATE   ZIP

Terms and prices subject to change. Your enrollment subject to acceptance by Silhouette Books.

SILHOUETTE ROMANCE is a registered trademark.

CBR6T5

TAKE 4 FREE SILHOUETTE ROMANCE NOVELS

Plus a Mystery Gift FREE! →

ment open, swiftly crossed the foyer and locked the
outside entry before tapping softly at his door in case
he had come home without her knowing it. After a few
moments she selected the correct key, fitted it into the
lock and turned it.

It was dark in Nolan's room, but she didn't turn on
the lamp. Instead she navigated by the light from the
foyer and the moonlight that filtered in through the
tree outside the west window and splashed interesting
designs upon the chenille bedspread and floor. A pair
of jogging shoes rested side by side in the midst of a
patch of moonlight at the foot of the bed Mary Judith smiled at them and scanned the room, her eyes
now adjusted to the darkness.

Nolan Tanner had a penchant for neatness, she decided. The room was in surprisingly good order. It
seemed to hold an essence of him, the aroma and feel
of his presence. She felt oddly content, at peace, despite the turmoil of the morning and evening. Sighing
deeply, she sat down on the sofa that flanked the bed,
settled into its corner and drew her feet up beneath
her. For the first time she wondered where he was and
why he had been gone so long. He needed his rest, and
they had so much to talk about. She hoped he would
be home soon, but it didn't matter. However long, she
would wait.

It was well past midnight when he came in. She was
tired and must have slept, but the sound of his key
scraping in the entry lock brought her wide awake and
upright. His slow footsteps halted and then quick-
ened as he spotted the open door of his apartment and
crossed the foyer. He paused in the doorway, framed
by the light spilling into the darkened room. She held
her breath as she stood, a shadow rising against the

dappled moonlight. He stared at her for a moment, then pocketed his keys and stepped into the room, a cautious reluctance giving his movements more emphasis than normal.

"You're up late," he said. No greeting, no apologies, no questions. She let out her breath.

"I was worried about you."

"I told you not to be." He crossed to the table and emptied his pockets as if preparing to go to bed. Mary Judith fidgeted. The room seemed suddenly quite small and airless.

"I...are you all right?"

"Of course I'm all right. I'm tired, that's all. Been a long day." He walked around the end of the sofa and sank down onto the bed with a sigh. Leaning forward, he began to loosen the ties on his work boot.

"You said you wouldn't be gone long," she reminded him, irritated that she sounded petulant and whining.

"I lied," he admitted flatly, and his boot hit the floor with a clunk. He straightened, leaned back against his elbows and stared up at her. "Look, I had work to do, something that wouldn't wait. That's the way it is in this business. Everything has to be done on schedule. One fellow depends on the next to do his thing and get out of the way. Well, I had some details to clear up so the carpet people can get in there tomorrow." He sat up and bent over the second boot. "I didn't feel like explaining it at the time."

She smiled down at the back of his head. "You didn't want me to feel bad because you spent the whole day putting up my bookcase and then had to do your own work at night." He flung out his hands, then went back to untying his bootlace.

"Okay. I didn't want you to feel bad because I spent the whole day putting up your bookcase. Now I suppose you feel guilty and I'll have to spend the rest of the night talking you out of it, except that I just don't have the energy for it." He tugged at the other boot ineffectually. She went down on her knees, brushed his hands away and went to work loosening the ties.

"I'm feeling guilty all right," she told him, "but you can't talk me out of it. I'll have to do that myself." She slipped the boot from his foot, gathered up the other and sat them side by side beneath the bed. When she looked up again, he was staring at her, half of his face in shadow, half of it gently lit, a question in the one sparkling eye not hidden by the darkness. She sank back on her heels, folded her hands in her lap.

"I was wrong about you," she said. "A statement was made out of context, and I let it convince me that you were the sort of man, well, the sort of man I didn't want to become involved with, the sort that can't be trusted. Oh, I'm not sure that I ever really believed it. How could I? The way you are with Laine, with Marta—with me—the sort of man I thought you were couldn't be that way." She cocked her head to the side, wondering briefly where it was coming from, the poise, the sureness. She smiled wistfully. "I think I wanted to believe it in a way, as a defense against what I was feeling." She locked her gaze to his, allowing him the opportunity to read her eyes. "I'd forgotten how scary it is to fall in love."

He stared at her with wide eyes, while his lips slowly parted and his hand drifted up between them as if he wanted to reach out to her, then he changed his mind and swiftly moved his hand to the back of his neck.

"You don't pull any punches, do you?" His voice was strong but a little breathless. She could tell she'd shocked him. He leaned forward so that the light fell fully on his face, his forearms resting upon his thighs, hands linked. "You're right of course. Falling in love is scary, and I just have to wonder if we're ready for this."

She shook her head stubbornly. "Speak for yourself, Nolan. Don't try to lump my feelings in with yours. I'm not inexperienced, Nolan. I've been in love before, very much in love, and I've wondered if I ever could be again." She went up on her knees then and reached out to lay her hand against his cheek, a small, very tender smile gently curving her lips. "Now I know," she whispered. "Now we both know."

"Judith." He knew he shouldn't touch her, shouldn't kiss her. She was trying to change the whole focus of his life, threatening to upset his very carefully laid plans. But there she was, so lovely he ached from looking at her, that luscious mouth turned up at the corners and just offering itself to him. He shouldn't, but he couldn't think, not with her kneeling there, looking at him with her heart in her eyes like that, wanting him.

His hands went out, slipped beneath her arms, which came up then and circled his neck. He pulled her to him, lifted her gently, found her mouth, felt it widen to fit his, settle into place. The world just went crazy then. It tilted over on its axis, spun around, left him on his back on the bed with her in his arms. She was all softness, all puff and down and incredible woman, almost without substance, it seemed, except for the mouth that met his so hungrily, yielded and parted and accommodated the thrust of his tongue and then thrust back at him, demanding equal pleasure, offering equal passion.

He rolled her onto her side, felt her stretch out against him, meeting his hard, tense planes with full, rounded curves. His hand had slipped down to her waist, rested now against the curve of her hip, and there at his fingertips, covering them, was the hem of her blouse. That hand just naturally pushed upward, her flesh warming his palm as it traveled her body and closed on the incredible softness of her breast. There was more to her than he had imagined, and some of it as firm as parts of his own body, but all of it woman, intensely female.

He heard a moan, thought it had come from him, and then realized it was her, reacting to the firm kneading of his hand. It was not the first time a woman had given voice to the sensations he had aroused in her, but it *felt* like the first time, complete with the wonder and the temerity and the overwhelming mystery of the force that compels men and women to join. It felt like the first time and suddenly he believed it was. He had no memory of another time, another woman. There was only now and this woman and the want of her throbbing in his groin. He had a sudden vision of her rising up to meet him, the lids fluttering down over those incredible green eyes as he pounded their bodies together. He wanted to make her sing out with the ecstasy of it.

"Nolan." He heard his name and broke away to smile against the graceful column of her throat before sinking his teeth into it ever so tenderly. "Nolan, where's mommy?" Suddenly he recognized that voice, and it wasn't Judith's. They exploded apart, ricocheting off each other in the quiet scramble to get the world back on its axis.

"Here I am, darling," said Judith, springing up from the bed. Laine stood in the doorway, rubbing her eyes with her fists. Mary Judith hastily smoothed her hair and clothing and went to her daughter, stooping to catch her up in her arms. Laine laid her head on Judith's shoulder and closed her eyes, oblivious of the scene she had just broken up and the turmoil resulting from that timely interruption.

Nolan hovered at the edges of the shadows and tried to compose himself. When Judith turned to him and whispered, "I'm sorry," he shook his head.

"No. That was my fault. I never meant to..."

She hushed him with a hand pressed against his chest.

"I'd better get her back to bed."

He nodded, his heart thudding against her palm. "We all need to get some sleep." She smiled at him gratefully, as if he'd released her from a promise she hadn't meant to make and couldn't keep.

"Will I see you in the morning?" she asked, and he knew he ought to say no. He had work to do, and she might as well get it straight now that the work had to come first. But he heard himself saying the exact opposite of what he'd meant to.

"Sure." He wanted to take it back, but he couldn't. He just couldn't. "I have to be out of here by eight," he said, as if that cleared up everything. She nodded and shifted the sleeping Laine into a more comfortable position.

"Good night," she whispered, smiling so happily he hated himself.

He closed the door behind her and dropped onto the bed fully clothed, but she was sleeping peacefully before he finally succumbed to dreams of soft feminine curves and a voice that cried out his name at the most appropriate of moments.

Mary Judith sent Laine early the next morning to see if Nolan was interested in breakfast—and held her breath until he was seated at the table in her kitchen, some ten minutes later. Both of them were awkward and self-conscious about the events of the evening before, and Judith knew only one thing for certain: she was in love with Nolan Tanner.

His feelings seemed more ambiguous but were perhaps best expressed by the hesitancy in his smile and the timidity of his gaze. She realized that she had put him in a difficult situation by declaring her love and that he was under no obligation to return those feelings, but she also rememberd the very real passion that had exploded between them and she sensed that his emotions, if confused, were as intense as her own. She tried to ease the situation as best she could by being her usual warm, friendly self.

Before long they were laughing at some silly thing Laine had said, and a little while later when she got up to fill his coffee cup, he rather casually put his arm about her waist. Laine immediately displayed a round-eyed curiosity, which he seemed not to notice as he raised the cup to his lips, sipped the dark liquid and nodded a compliment to Mary Judith, who gave her daughter a small, secretive smile. The whole scene had a homey air about it, a "family" feeling that seemed right and good and natural. It was all she could do to keep from kissing the sleek top of his head as she stood there with a glass carafe of coffee in one hand and the other placed lightly upon his shoulder.

He drank about half the cup, put it aside and only then noticed the stare of the six-year-old sitting across the table from him. At once his demeanor changed. He stiffened and slowly dropped his arm. His gaze shortened, lowered, regained its original reticence. Mary Judith self-consciously moved from his side and replaced the carafe on the warming tray. Laine's brow creased, and after a brief moment she excused herself to go and brush her teeth.

"Nolan?" Judith queried carefully, coming back to take her seat. "Can we talk about what's wrong?"

He toyed with the handle of his coffee cup. "Well, I'll tell you what it isn't." He lifted his gaze then, and it was warm and frank. "It isn't the beautiful, desirable woman who seems to be in love with me." He reached across the table for her hand.

She returned his grip, gently correcting him. "Is," she insisted, "not *seems*." He smiled.

"Okay."

She added her free hand to the knot of fingers on the table. "So tell me," she urged. "If it's not me, what is it?" His gaze shifted abruptly to his cup, and he gently slipped his hand from her grasp.

"Me," he said after a pause. "It's me, Judith. It's the mess I've made of my life, the things I have to do now to make it right, the people I owe, innocent people who lost money on me." He sighed and turned the cup around on its saucer. "It's a lot of things, honey, but it's mostly time."

"Time? How so?"

He swiveled around in his chair, facing her, his knee pressing against hers, his hands seeking hers again.

"Judith, Judith, honey, try to understand this. I have to work especially hard right now, not just to support myself. I can do that. But to raise money to pay back all those people who got hurt because they trusted me." He lifted a hand to his temple. "It's complicated, and I don't have time now to fully explain it, and that's a large part of the problem." He paused to draw breath, and Mary Judith jumped in.

"Nolan, I understand more than you think, and I'm so proud of what you're doing. You didn't cheat any of those people. They worked for you because they trusted you, and what you're doing now confirms that trust, but you didn't cheat them, and everyone who knows the facts understands that."

He sat up straight in his chair, hooked an arm over its back and grinned at her. "Well, well. Seems I underestimated you. But where did you come by all these endearing conclusions? The newspapers didn't exactly make a point of exonerating me, you know. I mean, they fell short of questioning my innocence outright, but neither did they give me a clean bill of health. You're either reading between the lines—quite liberally, I might add—or you've done some investigating on your own."

His grin broadened, and she had the distinct impression that he would have been flattered had she done what he was suggesting she'd done. It was then that she realized her mistake. A chill blew over her, and she dropped her gaze to their linked hands, trying to believe that a single omission of information would not adversely affect what they had going for them. Inside, though, she knew it wasn't the omission; it was the information itself.

"Nolan, darling, there was something I should've mentioned last night. I, I guess I just forgot. Things seemed to get out of hand so quickly..." She glanced upward, saw the concern and discomfort in those dark eyes and completely misread it. She gulped, fearing the worst and felt her courage quickly draining away.

"That was my fault, Judith," he said quietly, and she turned a sharp look on him, suddenly confused. He went on in a hushed, almost contrite voice. "I didn't mean to escalate things like that. I was tired and feeling rather protective of you because of the accident; and, well, lady, you've been driving me crazy for weeks! Then out of nowhere you hit me with all this talk about love. I just sort of lost control, if you know what I mean, and I think you do. Fact is, Judith, if Laine hadn't come in when she did..."

He actually blushed, and it was such a sweet reaction that she wanted to throw her hands about him and hold on tight. Instead she lifted a hand to his face and stroked the backs of her knuckles against the cleanly shaven line of his jaw.

"What is it with you, Tanner?" she teased. "Do you always have to take the credit for everything? In case you didn't notice, I instigated that whole happy scene last night, and I'm not the least bit sorry."

He leaned forward and kissed her, his mouth fitting hers so perfectly she couldn't help thinking they were made for each other, meant to be lovers. How could she ruin that delicious moment? And what did it matter, anyway, that his father had stopped by while he was gone? People dropped in on one another all the time. That one little incident couldn't change things between them any more than it already had, and now was just clearly not the time to discuss it.

Nolan slowly pulled his mouth away and gazed down at her. "I don't want to hurt you, Judith. That's why you must understand right from the start how it has to be. I have to direct my energies toward my financial situation right now. Once that's rectified, then we can concentrate on us. Until then, we've got to go slow, honey, one step at a time. Agreed?"

She looked into those warm brown eyes and knew she'd promise him anything he asked. "We won't get in the way, Nolan," she told him. "We just want to love you. Laine and I just want to love you."

He stood and gathered her into his arms and held her for a long time, thinking how refreshingly honest she was, how frank and fearless. He couldn't tell her that he was afraid. He couldn't tell her how he feared for them, all of them, Laine as well as Judith and himself. Life was laid out in a certain path for him, and he wondered if he even had a right to drag a woman and a child along with him. He wondered if they could be happy with that part of himself that he was free to give. In all fairness he ought never to have allowed this to start. He hadn't meant to. But he felt so *alive* with Judith and Laine, so *wanted*. Wasn't that what she had said about the man with whom she would share her life, that he would be a man she wanted rather than a man she simply needed? As wrong as it might be, he couldn't help wanting to be that man.

They made a habit of having breakfast together. During those next couple of weeks it was oftentimes their only contact during the busy day. His general reticence seemed to have dispelled, but an increasing preoccupation took its place. Even as he forked eggs and bacon into his mouth, he seemed to be thinking of something else, but Judith didn't mind as long as it kept the awkwardness at bay. She shouldn't have, because his thoughts were mainly of her and her generosity.

Actually he spent a good deal of time trying to tell himself that he wasn't taking advantage of her, but it is difficult for an especially proud man to accustom himself to taking even that which is freely given without giving in return. And there was the rub: how to balance the relationship. It meant, of course, spending more of that most precious commodity—time.

He sat at her table one morning enjoying a second cup of coffee after a breakfast of waffles and apple sauce floated in melted butter and syrup and knew what he had to do. As his eyes roamed the room, he thought of all the things he could change or fix or add. In his mind he was busy, visualizing all that was involved. At times, however, he paused to simply watch her as she moved about the kitchen, putting away dishes, wiping the counter tops. With her every movement, he thought to himself how lovely she was, more than lovely, really. There was a purity about her, a wholesomeness—as hackneyed as that word had become—that had made him wonder more than once if she could be too good to be true.

But that was before he had held her in his arms and kissed her and sensed in her the stirrings of a passion as intense and sensual as any man could hope for. He had felt her response and looked into her eyes and known at once that she was for real, more real than any other woman had ever been to him. Was this contentment, this feeling that enveloped him as he watched her? Contentment or longing? If it were possible, he would say it was both.

He smiled at the train of his thoughts and purposefully switched tracks, this time going beyond the one room to consider and picture the repairs and enhancements he could manage in the rest of the house.

Mary Judith leaned against the counter, her arms folded across the waistband of her faded jeans. Laine had finished her breakfast and scampered off to brush her teeth. In a few minutes it would be time to take her to school. Mary Judith hated to leave while he sat there, palming his cup and smiling in that gentle, satisfied way.

He lifted his cup to his mouth and sipped from it, his eyes busy over its rim. Then they seemed to snag on something just beyond her and become riveted there. She watched as he set aside the cup, pushed away from the table and stood. He walked toward her but without really looking at her, not even as he drew near, and then he reached behind her and she turned, realizing that what commanded his attention was a lopsided cabinet door that had swung open behind her left shoulder. It was her "miscellaneous cabinet." The door hung off balance, no longer fitting the opening. She was forever shutting it, but it never stayed that way.

Nolan tried the door, swinging it experimentally and lifting it from the bottom. The lower hinge was loose; she could have told him that. He swung the door wide, reached inside and extracted a screwdriver she had stored there next to the empty butter containers and plastic bags. He fitted the screwdriver into the screw that held the hinge plate to the cabinet and turned it.

"Screw wasn't put in straight," he muttered. "Wobbled out a hole. There's nothing to hold it anymore." Finally he looked at her. "Got any white glue?" Mary Judith nodded, her brow furrowed with inquiry; yet she said nothing as she stepped closer and rummaged through the cabinet for the bottle of glue she kept there. Nolan took it from her hand. "Now I need a match stick, a wooden match stick."

While she went to get one from the tin box nailed to the wall above the old gas stove, he extracted the screws from the hinge where it connected to the cabinet. When she offered the match, he took it, struck it and blew out the flame as soon as the head had fully ignited; then he cleaned the blackened tip with his pocketknife. Next he carefully coated the end and sides of the match stick with the glue before inserting it into the hole in the cabinet. When he had pushed it in as far as it would go, he simply broke off the remaining end. The hinge plate went back up and the screw was inserted into the old hole, now filled with the matchstick. This time, when he fitted the screwdriver into the head of the screw and turned it, the screw bit into solid wood. When it had been properly tightened, he wiped away the glue that had oozed out of the hole and replaced the screwdriver.

Mary Judith couldn't believe the simplicity of the repair. She tried the door, delighted and amazed.

"Do you know how long I've had to put up with that lopsided door?" Nolan grinned, obviously pleased with himself.

"Just takes a little know-how," he explained, stepping to the sink to wash the glue from his fingers. She handed him a small towel and he dried his hands.

She turned back to the cabinet. "Look at it! I've put up with that thing for three years and you fixed it in less than three minutes. Mr. Tanner, you are one handy man to have around the house."

He smiled at her and handed back the towel. "Mrs. Vickers, you are one fine cook."

"Sounds like a good match to me, the cook and the handyman."

"We could go into domestic service."

Mary Judith laughed. The idea of Nolan Tanner as a domestic servant was absolutely ludicrous. "Oh, you'd be great at that," she teased. "I'm sure there's a huge demand for butlers who can rehang cabinet doors." He put on an indignant face.

"I'll have you know my expertise extends far beyond breaking off match sticks in holes. For instance, that tear in the vinyl over there, I can patch it." He thumped his chest with his thumbs. "And this drippy faucet, all it needs is a couple of washers. Oh, and I can fill and paint over the chip in the ceramic on the sink, and this window sash, this window sash needs...?"

"I get the idea!" Mary Judith threw up her arms, her voice filled with laughter and good humor. "You are a man of many talents."

"Mary," he affirmed, and proceeded to demonstrate one of them by stepping closer and encircling her shoulders with his arms. Warmth immediately surrounded her along with a feeling of belonging, of being in the right place at the right time with the right man. She lifted her chin, and he gently covered her mouth with his own. Her eyes fluttered shut and she melted against him. It was always like this when he kissed her. It was as if her body made music, as if it rose and twirled and lilted to the sweet, silent notes of an extraordinary love song.

She longed to be alone with him, really alone, in some quiet, private place where time could be suspended for a while and they could simply be together. But that never seemed to be the case. He was always on his way somewhere, always hurrying even when he wasn't, or else he was exhausted and could barely keep his eyes open. There were only these moments stolen out of time, these brief moments of silent music.

She told herself that it was enough—for now—but when he finally lifted his head and his mouth no longer brought that gentle pressure to hers, she knew they would never be enough. And sometimes, when he slowly pulled away from her and that look of longing was on his face, she thought he felt they needed more time together, too. Still, he had said that they should take it slowly, and she had agreed. She would not press him, and she wasn't ready to give up—not yet—not by a long shot. And in the meantime there were those lovely fragments of song.

Chapter Seven

Mary Judith Vickers was a patient woman, and that virtue never served her better than in those first few weeks of autumn. Summer was slowly fading. The days were still long and languid and warm, but a crispness had begun creeping into the nights, and in that first moment after the full weight of darkness had slipped into place, one could smell the distant coming of winter in the air. It brought visions of cozy evenings spent before the fireplace, evoked the remembered perfumes of cinnamon and hot apple cider and popcorn and nuts roasted in sugared oil, and made one pine for the holidays. It was a good time to be in love, even if it was a little lonely.

Oh, Nolan was there, even more than she had expected. At first, she had wondered if this new proprietary zeal of his was a good idea. He worked too much already. Daytimes he spent remodeling an increasing number of various buildings, almost all of them older homes like the boardinghouse. He no longer worked alone, however. More and more of his time was spent directing the work rather than actually performing it, and he often divided himself between two or more different crews and projects in a single day. The nights were reserved for the designing and "packaging" of new job proposals and for the meeting of prospective clients. Still, he somehow found time to putter around the house.

It was nothing at all for him to breeze in at ten o'clock in the evening to caulk the bathtub, or for midnight to find him replacing warped shelves in the pantry or putting the last coat of paint on the rebuilt back steps. Mary Judith, and sometimes Laine if the hour was propitious, would sit and watch him work or help out in some nominal way, and nine times out of ten there would be a halfhearted, good-natured argument over who bore the actual cost of repairs and renovations. Mary Judith knew he always understated the price of materials, but he would not admit it or allow her to cancel or reduce his rent. She always lost those arguments and that bothered her, but he seemed to enjoy his little projects so she let him go on with it. She even wondered, hopefully, secretly, if he were not in a way making this place his own.

As for her, she performed a high-wire act, balancing between the roles of proper landlady and woman in love. She cooked his meals, laughed at his antics, secretly wept at the tenderness with which he handled Laine and was very careful that the other tenants had nothing about which to gossip.

But even this nearly idyllic time had its awkward moments, like the day he stormed in, threw his blueprints and clipboard at the kitchen table and announced that he had made the most colossal mistake of his career, something about weight barriers and cutting at the wrong angles. She didn't understand it. She only knew that the crisis could not be as severe as he made it sound. She said something about mistakes being part of life and that the manner in which one resolved them was ultimately all that could be controlled. He left still angry and predicting that he would lose his shirt—again. But that evening he brought her a bouquet of cut flowers and thanked her for her levelheaded response to his outburst.

Later, after he'd spent a few minutes reading to Laine and then helped her mother tuck her in, they talked about the frustrations of the business and how he'd finally found a solution for this latest catastrophe. He told her that he'd had his doubts about the design from the beginning, but that the client had insisted so he'd gone ahead.

"A year ago I wouldn't have let some joker talk me into this, but a year ago I wasn't desperate, either."

"Desperation is a state of mind, Nolan," she pointed out. He stretched, his arms pushing along the back of the sofa.

"Yeah, I know." He relaxed, and one arm fell at his side, while the other quite naturally draped itself about her shoulders. "Sometimes I wonder what the heck it's all about," he admitted. "I try to think it out rationally, but the only conclusion I ever come up with is that I've got to do it. I've got to get back to a place where I feel comfortable. I suppose it has to do with the way I was raised, the kind of Highland Park upbringing I had."

Highland Park was perhaps the most exclusive neighborhood in the Dallas area. A city unto itself, it maintained strict building and maintenance codes and uniformly high property values. Its schools were among the finest in the nation, its community pride awesome. Mary Judith supposed that being raised in such an environment might foster dissatisfaction with what one found in the rest of the world.

"Were you so happy there?" she asked, half fearing the answer. He looked at her, mild surprise arching his brows.

"Actually, Judith, I'm not quite certain I've ever been really happy anywhere. And maybe that's the problem. Maybe I'm never going to be satisfied because I just don't know how to be." It seemed a sad commentary on his life, and it made her sorry she had asked, until he smiled and nudged her nose with his own and whispered, "You know, honey, moment to moment, I'm happier when I'm with you than at any other time."

Moment to moment, she thought, day to day, week to week, month to month, year to year. Slowly but surely she was gaining ground. Slowly but surely she was winning. She had to be. She just had to be.

She leaned her head against his shoulder and reached up with one arm to encircle his neck. She wanted to say that she loved him, but the few times she had done so had brought only a bittersweet response. She had almost decided that the next time those words were said, he should be the one saying them. But meanwhile there was all that love inside of her, and in moments like these it seemed to swell and build to a pressure point, just as steam builds in a teakettle, and she desperately needed some way to express it, some way to let off the pressure.

She moved her hand to the back of his head and turned her face up, seeking his mouth. He bent to her with such eagerness it surprised her. His usual reticence seemed to have failed him for once, and she found that a little disturbing but also terribly exciting. She felt the desire burgeoning in him, and it was so wonderfully mutual, so fresh and sharp and intense and so full of love, so very full of love.

He leaned heavily against her shoulder, and his hand slipped down to her hip. Gently he turned her to her side, and they slowly sank down together upon the couch, face to face, their mouths joined, their arms tightening about one another. The space was narrow, affording them an excellent excuse to cling together, their legs entwined, hands roaming to press at strategic places.

He had kissed her like this once before, and even as the memory of those sensations came flooding back to her, he provided new ones to crowd them out. The manipulations of his mouth were frenetic, as if he wanted to devour her, and she was unashamedly willing to accommodate him, parting her lips to the hot, probing tip of his tongue. She was keenly aware of every separate sensation, the heat that scorched the roof of her mouth, the silkiness against the sharp edge of her teeth, the subtle pull of firm, spare lips. But the sensations were not confined to that kiss.

She became aware suddenly of his hand at her hip, his fingertips extending just beneath the hem of her blouse where it had pulled free of the waistband of her jeans. The bare skin tingled where his fingers rested against it and then prickled with a rush of heat as his hand pushed upward along her rib cage and closed over the soft mound of her breast. The muscles of her abdomen tightened as bolts of electricity shot through her, and her spine arched, pulling her head back. He nipped the tender flesh beneath her chin, then moved upward to trace the curve of her earlobe with the tip of his tongue. Waves of chills racked her body, followed quickly by a hot, moist contraction in her belly.

Then, as his mouth followed the line of her jaw and began a slow descent of the smooth column of her throat, he moved his hand to the front of her blouse and quite deftly slipped each button. He kissed her as he laid the front of her blouse open, his mouth capturing and holding hers as he pushed away the strap at her shoulder. He lifted his head then and looked at her, a silent question in those dark, glittering eyes, as he covered her naked breast with his palm. It was the same: electric jolts simultaneous with that clutching tightness deep inside her abdomen, the arching against him that emphasized the hard ridges and rills of his body. She was aware of nothing else until she felt the tip of his tongue flicking heat over the turgid peak of the naked globe and then his mouth enveloped her and she cried out the one word left in her memory, his name.

It was as if she'd unleashed something formidable within him. Suddenly his mouth was taking hers again and again and again, never satisfied, always yearning, demanding. His hands were everywhere, in her hair, at her face, her breast, following the dip at her waist and rounding the curve of her hip, crossing the flat of her abdomen, stroking her thigh. It seemed that all she could do was hold on and reel with each successive blast of exquisite sensation. She could no longer think, no longer reason, and only that one beloved word came to her lips. It was the single refrain of her song, the lyric that inspired the music, and her heart sang it in joyful abandonment.

Then it was that she heard the first discordant note. It came to her as if from a great distance and yet sounded very near. It was a grating, a series of metallic clicks and scrapes. No music this, but suddenly, wrenchingly familiar. It was the sound of a zipper slowly separating, the sound of thoughtless surrender to a mindless passion born of an unproven love. It was the warning clarion before the final act of commitment. But commitment to what? A lifetime loving a man who had not yet demonstrated a clear understanding of the word? An eternity wanting a partner who might never completely join with her?

She reached out quite purposefully and stayed his hand, surprised at the strength she found in her grip and the almost instant clarity of her mind. He stiffened and lowered his head to her shoulder, his breath coming in quick, shallow flurries, then he levered his weight onto his side, wedging his body between hers and the back of the sofa.

Mary Judith slipped the strap over her shoulder and gathered her blouse together. She slowly sat up and slid from the edge of the couch onto her knees. Carefully she righted her clothing, then sat on the floor with her legs curled at her side, her hands straying up to her hair.

"Judith?"

She fixed her gaze on him, held it even and long. In her mind were a dozen things to say, but only one really mattered, the one that went right to the heart.

"Nolan, do you love me?" she asked.

He pushed up from the couch and brought his feet to the floor. Sitting with elbows on knees, he rubbed his hands over his face and looked down at her.

"Judith..." He seemed to be struggling with the words. "Never in my life have I needed a woman as much as I need you." He shook his head. "No, that's not exactly what I meant to say...It's that, well, that I've never had time to think about love and suddenly even when I don't want to be I'm thinking about you." He spread his hands, pleading with her to understand what he himself could not. "I want to be with you. I *need* to be with you. Is that love, Judith? Is it?"

She had no ready answer for him, just as he had had none for her. Even now there were only questions. She tossed her head.

"Is it safe to say that you care about me, Nolan?"

"Absolutely."

"And Laine?"

"You know I do."

She leveled her gaze at him. "Do you care enough to make us a family, enough to marry me?"

His breath caught and his face, on which there was a shadow of a beard, paled. He leaped to his feet and strode past her, halting with his hands pressed to his hips, the fingertips coming together in the small of his back. She reached for the edge of the couch and pushed up to a standing position, a foreboding filling her.

"Judith." His voice was strangled and deep. "You know this isn't the time for that." He turned his head and glared at her, his eyes filled with accusation. "You know I can't even *think* of marriage now."

"And why not?"

Suddenly he rounded on her. "You know why! I made that perfectly clear. I don't have any choice in the matter; I have to concentrate on my work!"

"To the exclusion of all else?"

"Yes!"

"For how long, Nolan? Until you've very nobly paid back all those people who were cheated out of their money?" He stiffened as if she'd caught him unawares, and she found that extremely odd. "What is it? What..." The question died as the answer became suddenly clear. She stared at him, unable to believe that he hadn't shared this with her. "It's finished, isn't it? You're through with that."

"I paid off the last creditor a few days ago, if that's what you mean."

She gaped at him. "It's done? What you've been working for, it's done and you didn't even bother to mention it? Why, Nolan? Why?"

He flung out a hand lamely. "I've just been so busy. There's so much else to do."

"Like what?"

He glared at her. "Like getting the business off the ground!"

"You've done that already," she pointed out stubbornly.

"But there's a long way to go yet! It's nothing like before. We're still a small-time operation. We need capital to make investments. We need bigger and better projects. We need offices and staff and a formal charter. And someone has to make all that happen!" Agitated, he shook his fists at the ceiling. "For Pete's sake, Judith, do you expect me to live my whole life in a boardinghouse?"

Her chin came up sharply. "I have!" she snapped, and he winced as if she'd slapped him. "Is that it, Nolan?" she went on in a bitter, quavering voice. "Is it that we're just not good enough for you?"

"You know I didn't mean that."

"I don't know anything of the kind." She did. She knew from the look in his eyes that he hadn't meant it as a put-down. She knew he was hurting at that very moment because he'd hurt her, but it was more than a carelessly phrased sentence. She had her pride, too, after all, and she didn't ask a man to marry her every day of the week. It didn't help that his reason for refusing was simply that he couldn't take the time to do it! And when she thought of that scene on the couch, when she thought that he'd have taken her right then and there if she'd allowed it...She hadn't believed he would do that. Somewhere deep within her naive little heart she hadn't believed he would do it! She pivoted and strode around the end of the couch to the door. Her cheeks were flushed when she yanked it open and turned to face him. "I think you'd better get out."

She saw the nostrils flare, the wide shoulders lift and square, the strong hands coil into fists, but she would not be intimidated. Let him be angry. Let his pride smart and suffer. She had a right to her own rage, her own affrontery. It wasn't supposed to be like this. They had talked, established the rules. He'd set a gallant, honorable goal for himself, and she'd loved him because of it, but once it was achieved, it was supposed to be her turn. And he hadn't even bothered to tell her when it was done!

He strode toward her, fists clenched, a muscle working in the blue-tinged hollow of his jaw, and despite her anger she couldn't help thinking that he was walking out of her life. She saw her dreams going out that door with him, saw Laine's sad little face and the questions in those big guileless eyes, and it was all so damned unfair!

He reached for the door and she turned her face away, determined to let him go but totally unable to watch it happen. She heard the slam, the final, jarring salvo in a war nobody had won, and something in her gave way. It was like the breaking of a dam, and she felt the first sweeping rush of an all too familiar flood of sorrow and grief.

"Look at me, Judith." The sound of his voice brought her around, eyes wide and wondering. She looked at him, saw the furrowed brow, the dark, gleaming eyes, the mouth set tautly above the proud thrust of his chin. His hand was pressed flat against the closed door; the other came up to clamp over the slope of her shoulder where her neck curved into it.

"You wanted a chance for us," he reminded her in a firm, husky voice, "and you made me want it, too. I don't give up on what I want. Even when I don't know exactly what it is, I can't quit until I have it. You've got to learn that about me, Judith. You've got to learn that you can't ask me to quit. Maybe I don't know what it is I'm really working for, but I do know that it's more than the money or the power or the prestige because I've had those things before and they just didn't make my life complete! Now maybe I can't have whatever it is I'm reaching for and you, too, but I'm not ready to give up on either one yet. Do you hear me, Judith? I'm not ready to give up!"

"I hear it. But, Nolan," she pleaded, "what about me? You know what almost happened tonight! I love you, but I have my pride. You can't expect me to..."

"I don't! But I won't apologize for what did happen, either!" He seized her suddenly and brought her hard against him, his face close to hers, his mouth a mere breath away. "You made me want you like this," he told her. "Don't blame me if you got more than you bargained for!" He crushed her against his body, one hand splayed at her hips, the other digging into her hair at the nape of her neck. His mouth hovered over hers, poised to take it, and—God help her—she could feel herself melting against him, feel the resistance crumbling, the passion flaring up to consume it.

She desperately wanted him to kiss her and knew that if he did she would be utterly lost. There would be no pulling back from it this time, nothing withheld, no strength left with which to give him up, no part of her which would not succumb to the compelling spell of mutual desire. Pride was nothing compared to such desire as she saw in those dark-brown eyes or that which rose up in her to meet it. Her own she could fight, or his, but not both of them together! She was a fool to have thought she could fight both and ever hope to win. And she was no longer even certain that she wanted to.

All right! Let it come! Love me! Please!

He must have read her thoughts, for it was then that she saw the glint of decision in his eye, felt his arms fall away, his hands at her shoulders firmly setting her aside. He reached for the doorknob, turned it, pulled and paused to fix her with a look full of reluctance and a kind of confused surrender. She stared at him, a thousand fearful questions in her eyes. He answered them with a gentle shake of his head.

"Do you think," he asked her softly, "that I could leave now if I *didn't* love you?"

He turned away, strode purposefully into the foyer. The tears were streaming down her face even before the door closed behind him.

She hardly saw him during the next four days, and each time it was with an apologetic smile on his face and a hurried word of explanation.

"Got to go, love. Prospective client."

"All hell's broken loose at the Avenue D site. I have to get over there and smooth things over."

"Sorry, sweetheart, the banker's expecting me first thing this morning."

"It's a meeting with a realtor. We'll be late."

"I've just *got* to make the changes in these plans tonight!"

"Blasted carpenter didn't show up. I'll have to finish the trim carpentry on the Ice House project myself."

"Tomorrow's payday, babe, so tonight I'm the accountant."

Then on Friday afternoon he walked in with a bunch of flowers wrapped in green waxed paper and a grin as wide as the Grand Canyon.

"You're looking at the builder of a new shopping center going up on Fort Worth Drive," he announced proudly. "Put on your party clothes, darlings, we're celebrating!"

He tacked notes and twenty-dollar bills on the doors of the two upstairs apartments while she dug the blue lawn dress out of her sewing basket, hastily finished the hem and pressed out the wrinkles. Half an hour later they congregated in the foyer, Nolan in a double-breasted navy-blue suit and a burgundy tie over a white shirt. Laine had traded her jeans and sneakers for orchid lace and white patent-leather baby dolls and added a bouncy bow to her ponytail. And then there was Mary Judith.

She watched his eyes light as she walked toward him, her hair loosely piled in a froth of curls atop her head and fastened with a pearly clasp. The muted flower print of the blue lawn swirled about the calves of her legs as she moved. The collarless bodice draped about her shoulders, dipping to a soft, unstructured V in the front. She wore it belted, with a long strand of pearls knotted between her breasts. The ends of a big crocheted shawl of lacy cream-colored wool hung gracefully in the crooks of her arms, just above the narrow cuffs at her wrists, where the long full sleeves gathered softly.

She had brought a dark-red rosebud from the bouquet to pin on his lapel, and while she did so, he drew her close and whispered that she looked like a walking dream and that with her on his arm he would be the envy of every man. Then Laine was pushing between them, begging to smell the rose, and he bent to sweep her up, his arm curled about the thin legs encased in white stockings.

The three of them squeezed into the sports car, Laine and Judith both clamped into one seat belt, and within the hour they were climbing a circular staircase to a posh Chinese restaurant in North Dallas. The maitre d' expressed great surprise and delight at seeing an obviously regular but long absent customer and waved aside apologies for a lack of reservations. He led them through a maze of small, softly lighted mauve and silver rooms to a quiet table beside a window with an enthralling view that was to be the focal point of Laine's evening.

The child sat mesmerized by the ever-changing picture through six types of appetizers, the table-side preparation and service of the soup course and a trio of main dishes, one of them a sizzling lobster cracked and drenched in a thick, spicy, dark sauce. She watched the street filled with traffic below and the winking on of lights as darkness transformed the character and appearance of the surrounding buildings, and she listened contentedly to the murmur of conversation and gentle laughter that came from the opposite side of the table where her mother and Nolan sat and smiled into each other's eyes. She remembered later being vaguely aware of the presence of another, but she remained unaware of the exact moment when the other man approached and really took note of him only when she caught the reflection of his frowning face in the night-backed window.

She thought it was Nolan at first, until she realized that the swatch of white that swept back from his forehead was not the glare of light upon the glass, and it was then she turned, out of curiosity, first to see her mother's pale face and then Nolan's angry one and finally to stare up into the dark solemn eyes of a very tall, very unhappy stranger.

"I'm sorry, Judith," he was saying to her mother. "It never occurred to me you wouldn't mention my visit, but I'm sure you did what you considered best. Please allow me to say how very lovely you are this evening. And Nolan, try to understand. I only wanted to see you to be certain that..."

"Oh, I can just imagine!" Nolan interrupted, and Laine looked at him in surprise.

"Morgan, please," her mother pleaded. "Let's not have a scene here."

The older man bowed slightly and attempted to smile. "Yes, of course. My apologies." He looked to Laine then, as if noticing her for the first time, patted her atop the head, cast her mother a last bewildering look and moved away. Nolan got up from the table and stalked from the room, his napkin lying in a heap upon the floor.

"Come on, honey," Mary Judith said softly, her voice trembling. "We have to go now." Laine was sure, as they wove their way through the tables, that she had seen tears in her mother's eyes, and she knew instinctively that something had gone wrong. But who could figure out adults?

Silence permeated the interior of the car on the way home. Mary Judith alternately stared out her window and at her daughter's little hands, one of which rested on Nolan's thigh and one of which rested on her own, as if that would somehow bridge the gulf that had opened between them. She was miserably aware of the fact that she had made a momentous mistake, and only Laine's subdued presence kept her from frantically stating her case and petitioning for understanding. Instead she prayed that his obvious anger would abate during the drive home and concentrated on what she would say to him after they arrived and Laine was in her room, safely out of earshot.

She could have saved herself the silent rehearsal. It became apparent soon after their arrival that he was interested in talking, not listening. He left her with Laine in the foyer, saying that he was going to change and give her a few minutes to take care of "things," then he expected to see her in his room, where he had a few choice words for her. More than a few, actually. Many more.

She tapped at his door a good forty-five minutes later, having taken as long as possible to settle Laine in front of the television and exchange the blue flowered lawn dress for a casual skirt and sweater. He called out to her to come in, and she opened the door, the effects of the past two hours weighing on her heavily.

He stood in the bathroom door, a towel draped about his naked shoulders, his feet bare beneath his jeans. His gleaming hair was swept straight back from the brow and plastered to his head, sharpening his features.

"I thought a cold shower might help lighten my mood," he told her cryptically.

"It doesn't appear to have," she replied, and he sent her a dark, glowering look.

"Your powers of observation are keen. But then we already knew that about you, didn't we? For instance, you observed that animosity exists between me and my father. Why else would you have deliberately kept from me the fact that the two of you had met to discuss me?"

Judith steadied her gaze and spoke purposefully, thinking through each word. "First of all, we didn't meet to discuss you. He came here one evening looking for you, and naturally he came to my door. I invited him in out of courtesy, and one thing led to another."

"You invited him in."

"Out of courtesy," she reiterated. He seemed to want to mull that over. He gripped both ends of the towel and strolled forward.

"You know, of course, that *I* wouldn't have invited him in—out of courtesy or anything else," he said.

She dropped her gaze guiltily. "I suspected as much."

"But *you* wouldn't dream of treating another person that way, would you?" he went on, his voice growing softer and huskier. "No matter what had passed between you." She looked up to find him standing very near, those coffee-brown eyes probing her face. He dropped one end of the towel and crooked his finger beneath her chin, tilting it slightly upward. "Why didn't you tell me?" he whispered, and she felt her lower lip begin to quiver.

"I just never could seem to find a time for it," she managed. Swallowing, she forced herself to go on, her heart beating with slow, forceful thumps against the walls of her chest. "At first, so many wonderful things were happening between us that it sort of got shunted aside. It didn't seem important. Then as time went on, I began to wonder when he was going to call or drop by again, and I knew that I had to tell you about that first visit, but I couldn't seem to find an appropriate time to drop it into the conversation. It was just one of those silly things you keep putting off until it's too late."

He searched her face a moment longer, as if trying to decide something, then he moved his hands to the back of her shoulders and gently massaged them.

"All right, but now you listen to me. I don't want that man in this house. I don't even want him to know anything about my business or my personal life. Do you understand that, Judith? I want him kept away from me."

He seemed to be offering her a deal. If she would agree to help him keep his father at arm's length, he would forgive her this one lie of omission. She wanted to be docile and submissive and agree. It was his life, after all, and his father. But the whole thing smelled to high heaven and she just couldn't bring herself to meekly acquiesce without understanding why he would ask such a thing of her.

Her head started to go up and down in agreement. Nolan's face drew together in a glower. Mary Judith sighed and shook her head.

"I'm sorry, Nolan, but I just don't get it. That man is your father, for pity's sake! He wants to see you, to be close to you. He loves you!"

He dropped his hands, stared at her for a moment as if she'd grown a second head and whipped the towel from around his shoulders.

"My father wouldn't know love if it walked up and punched his lights out! You want to know what being a father means to him? It means having a license to degrade and humiliate your kid. It means having someone to feel superior to. No wonder he wants to see me. I'm his own personal target for his ego!"

Judith couldn't believe they were talking about the same man. She had in her mind's eye the picture of an aging gentleman: contrite, defeated, hurting, but proud—so very proud, despite the alienation—of a son who wouldn't or couldn't accept his love. She remembered all the wonderful things he'd had to say about his son and the admission that he'd been a less-than-perfect parent. Was Morgan Tanner devious enough to pull off such a charade? Could he have purposely lied to her, told her what he knew Nolan wanted to hear? No. A person would have to be sick to do that, and Morgan Tanner, though unhappy, had seemed every bit as stable as his estranged son and somewhat resigned to his fate as the outcast father. She looked into those glossy chocolate eyes and knew that they were the ones wearing the blinders.

"Nolan, honey, wouldn't it be better if you and your father could sit down and talk out this problem once and for all? It couldn't hurt anything to try, and I have the feeling that there are some deep, unresolved resentments here that need ironing out."

His look was scathing, vehement. "Don't you understand, Judith? He'd just find some way to make me feel like a failure, and I can't handle that now, not after what I've been through!" He turned away from her and stalked about the room. "Look at what he's doing to us this very minute." He flung out his arms, shouting. "He doesn't even have to come around to mess up my life!"

His reaction stunned her. Didn't he know what he sounded like? It was as if the man she loved, that mature and responsible and gentle man, had suddenly reverted to adolescence, and all because she had met and talked with his father! He didn't even evidence any interest in the actual conversation, only the fact of his father's presence. He seemed stuck in that mindframe of adolescence when all adults and particularly parents are perceived as natural adversaries. If only he could see that his father actually loved and admired him. If only the two of them had learned to express their deepest feelings for each other. How sad, how heartbreakingly sad to have a living parent for whom one could never show love or appreciation. Suddenly she found herself yearning for her own parents, and that little-girl insecurity swept over her as the fact hit home once again that they were lost to her forever.

All at once, a light clicked on in her head. One moment she was suspended helplessly in a time warp of grief and vulnerability, and the next she was far above the scene, staring down at that small and lonely part of herself, and then she *knew* what Nolan Tanner was all about. He was a man struggling with a part of himself that had never been fully recognized or satisfied. He was a boy in the most confusing time of his life, a boy who had lost his mother and found himself living with a stranger who was also his father. He was a child railing inside against the unfairness and cruelty of life, an enigma to the only source of comfort and security he had. Inside that confident, determined, emotionally rich man lived two children, one who wanted to keep at bay the punisher and critic and disapprover and another who strove desperately to earn the rewards and praise and approval of a loving parent.

She looked at that beautiful man and saw the confusion and the turmoil going on inside of him, and at last she understood. What he needed now she could not give him. What he was striving for had been his all along. And he would never see it unless someone made him look deeply within himself at wounds still festering and raw. The prospect seemed suddenly overwhelming, and she had but one thought to cling to, one thought for him.

"We love you, Nolan," she told him, knowing that it sounded like capitulation. But "we" had grown to mean three people, herself, Laine and Morgan, and someday, somehow, he had to be made to see that or the fearful, insecure child in him would go right on keeping love at bay.

Chapter Eight

Mary Judith sat staring at the telephone and wondered if she ought to call Morgan or simply wait to see what happened next. It was so difficult to know what was best to do. On one hand, Nolan was an adult with every right to conduct his life as he chose. On the other, these unresolved animosities between son and father were overlapping, she felt certain, into her own life, and she was of no mind to sit idly by while Nolan chased after some vague, emotional goal that one childish part of him seemed reluctant to reach. Her love life was waiting for her at the end of that chase, and she ached for it to truly commence.

How did she ever get embroiled in someone else's emotional games, anyway? she wondered. The answer to that was obvious: by loving that someone in the first place. Love meant taking a person with all their foibles and hang-ups intact. Sometimes, during the inevitable friction that takes place when two people determine to keep on loving each other, those foibles and hang-ups prove to be rough spots that either get sanded down smooth or cause unremitting irritation. Either way, it takes two to tango.

It had been the same with Mick, of course. There had been problems, some small and some not so small, which had required direct attention. But it had happened gradually with Mick. It had taken a lot of rubbing against each other to find the snags, and even then they had emerged slowly over lengthy periods of time. But this love was different. It was as explosive as the passion that charged a casual display of affection with the dynamite of uncontrollable desire, the same force that found them warming their fingers one moment and scorching the skin off their bodies the next—and wondering how the heck the fire had gotten started in the first place.

With Mick, there had been security. She had risked nothing more than getting her feelings hurt if she tried to cure a tender spot with a heavier touch than required, but with Nolan she risked getting her heart shattered in tiny pieces, and she was keenly, dismally aware of that fact. It was this that kept her from picking up that phone, this that forced her to smile wanly and nod and pretend, as Nolan did, that Morgan Tanner and any discussion of him had simply never existed.

They pretended, but in reality she was shaking in her boots, just waiting for the ax to drop, while Nolan raced about like a madman. Where before he had worked seven days a week, he now worked eight, squeezing the extra hours from those too few set aside for sleep. Mary Judith began to worry about him. There never seemed to be a moment when he was at rest anymore, and consequuently each little project he plunged into around the house became a source of argument.

"You're the only woman I ever knew who wanted her house to fall down around her ears!" he would say, and she'd counter with something well thought out and reasonable like, "It's *my* house; I'll let it fall down if I want to!"

Moreover, since that night she'd practically let him make love to her on the living-room couch, they'd both been somewhat reticent about physical displays. Mary Judith realized that they were keeping each other at arm's length, and that playing handyman around the house was his way of trying to allow her equal time without risking any real entanglements, emotional or physical ones. She felt like she was gnashing her teeth on a steel bar. It all came to a head on Thanksgiving Day, when Nolan was too busy to even show up for dinner—and Morgan wasn't.

It started the morning before Thanksgiving, actually, when Mary Judith found Nolan asleep under her kitchen sink. The poor man had actually nodded off while trying to install a new drain trap before going to work. He'd gotten up early to do it, after too few hours of sleep, as usual, and nothing she could say would make him reconsider. She'd stuck around and tried to be of help for a while, but Laine was in a particularly petulant mood that morning and called her away time after time, until she'd given up and sat the child down for a long frank talk about her recent behavior.

The joint connecting the drain with the trap had put things on a temporary hold anyway. Nolan had struggled with it until he was physically exhausted. She had folded a rug and placed it strategically so that he was comfortable while he lay there, half in the cabinet and half out, and at the moment when she had gone to give Laine her richly deserved lecture, he was resting his arms, preparing to resume the war of the pipe wrench momentarily. Only the moment never came. Apparently all of him decided in that one unguarded instant to take a minivacation while the taking was good. When she returned, he was sleeping like Rip Van Winkle, and she didn't have the heart to wake him. As ridiculous as it seemed later on, she just threw a light cover over him and let him lay.

He was mad as hops when he woke after some two hours to find water dripping on his forehead. It seemed that Laine had sneaked into the kitchen and turned the faucet on to get a drink of water, despite her mother's clear instructions to the contrary, and that the joint had loosened just enough to form a tiny leak. They had a shouting match that lifted the roof and left the trap unfixed, all the while Laine, in tears, was clinging to her mother's skirt. The last thing he'd said as he stormed out of the house was that she'd made him lose so much time at work he'd probably be pounding nails on Thanksgiving Day. Sure enough, when she'd gone to his room the next morning to wake him for breakfast, he had already left and the prear-ranged two-o'clock dinner hour found her table oc-cupied by a single guest—Gilly, who never seemed to have anywhere else to go.

It was getting on to evening when Morgan Tanner showed up, his hat in his hand and a hopeful, sheep-ish expression on his face. He had a chocolate bar the size of Milwaukee in one pocket for Laine and a bot-tle of wine in the other for Judith. ''To make the leftovers more palatable," he said. She didn't even think about not inviting him in. Doing so would irritate Nolan.

She parceled out a smidgen of chocolate for Laine and cracked the bottle for herself and her guest. It was an excellent white wine chosen more for its pleasant taste than its suitability, but Mary Judith wouldn't have cared if it had been soda pop. All that mattered was that it gave her some reason to sit down and pretend that all was well. That lasted about five minutes. Then Morgan Tanner sat his glass on the coffee table and stared at her with peculiarly penetrating vision.

"Don't give up on him, Judith," he said quietly. "I can see that you're distraught, and the fact that he isn't here now tells me why. Hasn't he been here at all today?" She could only bite her lip and shake her head. He took up his glass again. "If you must blame someone, blame me," he said. "After all, he's only following the example I set for him. But we can't let him continue like this. Otherwise he'll wind up like me, old, rich—and lonely." He quaffed the last of the liquid and stared at the empty glass. It seemed symbolic somehow of the life he had made for himself and of the life Nolan seemed intent upon living. It was then that she realized her own glass would never be less than half-full because she at least had Laine, but Nolan and his father didn't even have each other.

Mary Judith made up her mind to enjoy the company at hand. She had been reaching out for Nolan for so long that she had almost forgotten there were other people in the world who needed a kind word and a moment of companionship, but no longer could she forget about others. Morgan Tanner was not her enemy, after all, any more than he was Nolan's, even if

Nolan insisted on casting him in that role, and she decided it was past time to confront the ghosts of the past—before they became the specters of the future, if it was not already too late.

Nolan found them in the living room when he finally dragged himself in at about eight o'clock. Mary Judith surmised later that he had had second thoughts about his behavior and was so intent upon apologizing that he hadn't even bothered to knock, because one moment she was laughing with Morgan about some silly tale from Nolan's childhood and the next the door opened and he came trudging in. He must have literally worked the anger out of his system because he was so exhausted there were big dark circles around his eyes, making him appear gaunt and pale. For the briefest moment she thought that he was going to miraculously accept what he saw there without a word. It seemed, at least in that moment, that the fight had just gone out of him. Then she saw the slow, reflexive straightening of his spine, the laborious lift of the shoulders and chin, and then he simply turned and walked out of the room.

Mary Judith leaped up and flew after him, eager for what she imagined to be this final cataclysmic confrontation, wherein they would all settle their differences and get happily on with the business of living and loving. But she hadn't yet come to understand the depth of that Tanner pride and the absolute stubbornness it could spawn. She followed him into his room, demanding that he listen to reason, and he ignored her. Without a word he pulled a suitcase from beneath the bed—that bed where he had held her and kissed her and first thought of loving her—and began to pack.

"What in blazes do you think you're doing?" she demanded, not yet succumbing to the shock of actually losing him. He glanced at her as if she was a person of no concern to him.

"I can afford a real apartment now," he informed her matter-of-factly. "I can even buy a house if I want." With that he abruptly abandoned the suitcase and walked into the bathroom. She could hear him gathering toilet articles and started after him, but he met her on the way, pushed past her and tossed a small black bag into the suitcase on the bed. He closed it and reached for the handle. The suitcase slipped from the bed and fell at his side.

"You can't just walk out!" she screamed at him, but he paused only long enough to fling her a hard, challenging stare.

"We want different things, Mary Judith. I want to rebuild my business and my career. I have to. It's what I'm all about." He shook his head. "I don't know what you want, but whatever it is, I just can't provide it. You proved that to me today."

"I want a husband!" she told him. "I want a husband and a lover, and a father for my child! I want you, Nolan, but you seem to think I'm asking you to give up something else in your life, and it's just not so!"

He shook his head stubbornly and tightened his grip on the handle of the suitcase. "I thought once that we could work out a compromise, Judith. I thought we had a chance, but you had to bring *him* into this. You just couldn't leave it alone, could you? Well, he's poison to me, lady. He's poison! Let me guess something. Let me guess that he was the source of your information about me, or should I say misinformation? He's the one who had you thinking I was a criminal, wasn't he?''

She felt the color drain from her face and rushed to qualify the obvious answer contained in her reaction. "That was my misunderstanding, Nolan!"

"Was it?" he sneered. "And did he also tell you how he rubbed my nose in what my partners were doing? How he saved the day by exposing them and making a laughingstock out of me in the process?''

She closed her eyes, knowing that she was fighting a losing battle. "He didn't put it that way, Nolan. That's your bitterness and wounded pride talking now!"

"Oh, I'm bitter," he admitted caustically. "I'm bitter all right, but not wounded, and I won't ever be again, not by him. I made up my mind a long time ago that that old man would never hurt me again. I won't let him get to me, no matter what or who he uses! That's the thing neither one of you seem to understand. The days are over when he can reduce me to a pile of jelly with a withering look or a snapped command. I'm not his punching bag anymore. I'm my own man, and that's the way it's always going to be!"
He'd said it all now, the flat, persistent denial of everything and everyone who even came into contact with Morgan Tanner—and that meant even those people he had learned to love. She knew that as certainly as she knew that somewhere beneath all those layers of resentment and confusion and anger lived still a love for his father. But it was a love Nolan could not face. "I'll send for the rest of my things in a few days," he said, and hauled his suitcase out into the foyer.

Mary Judith followed lethargically, numbed by the rejection of all that she and Laine had to give him, all the love and caring and patience and hope, all the unity and purpose and affection. He walked resolutely toward the door, and she knew that nothing she could say or do would stop him. And then he was simply gone, and a cup half-full seemed less than it had before.

When the shock finally subsided long enough to allow her to think, Mary Judith wandered back into the living room, where she found Morgan Tanner with his face in his hands.

"You heard?"

He dropped his hands and abruptly straightened, nodding. "Enough. Enough to know my son hates me." He stood and turned to her, his face wan and colorless. "I didn't realize...I didn't realize how terribly he..." On the verge of a breakdown, he halted and squared his shoulders forcefully. "You love him very much, don't you?" She nodded, her mouth firmed against the recurrent trembling of her lip. "I'm sorry!" he whispered, and covered his face again. She could see him breathing deeply and thought for a moment that the incredible Tanner pride would conquer once more. Then the tears began to drip between his fingers, and she went to him and put her arms about his shoulders.

The most difficult part of it all was yet to come, however: trying to explain to Laine why Nolan had so suddenly left them.

Mary Judith first decided to act casual about his departure. Tenants came and went frequently, she said. But Laine was not to be fooled by such triteness. She knew that Nolan Tanner had been much more to them than just a tenant. They had loved him, she pointed out, and he had just picked up and vanished without so much as saying goodbye. "Almost like my father," she added.

Mary Judith quickly pointed out that there was no correlation between Mick's "leaving" and Nolan's. She didn't want Laine to get the idea that every man she loved would invariably leave her, but Laine saw only one real difference: Mick had not wanted to go; Nolan had clearly chosen to do so.

Following that conclusion came the realization on Mary Judith's part that her daughter felt some genuine anger over Nolan's absence. This caused some moments of anxiety, but ultimately Laine's reaction seemed fairly typical.

"He didn't stay around here very much anyway," she groused philosophically. "But we got the house fixed up, didn't we?"

Mary Judith felt relieved. It seemed as healthy a reaction as any.

"You should never be friends with a person just because of what you can get from them," she carefully explained. "But we should certainly be thankful for all the nice things Nolan did for us while he was here. And you know, it's okay to say we're going to miss him, even though we didn't get to spend as much time with him as we would have liked."

Laine considered this for a second, her big dark eyes—so like Nolan's—narrowing as she weighed the argument, then she stubbornly shook her head. "Can't help it," she announced. "I'm not gonna miss him a bit!" Which meant, of course, that she definitely would. Her mother could only wish that saying it made it so.

They were not without solace, however. Marta surprised Mary Judith by quickly assaying the situation and privately offering a willing shoulder and an open ear. Moreover, she saw to it that the others kept their questions and comments to themselves. Even Trish, who couldn't have thought before she opened her mouth if she'd wanted to, managed to publicly ignore Nolan's leave-taking with grace and aplomb. Gilly, who Mary Judith suspected was secretly pleased with this turn of events, never said a word about Nolan's absence and yet was more jovial and chatty than ever. Then there was Morgan.

Morgan blamed himself for the situation every bit as much as Nolan blamed him, but Mary Judith was not willing to let that idea stand. Nolan was an adult man responsible for his own actions and attitudes. Everyone had to forgive the inequities of everyone else in this world, or there could be nothing but loneliness and bitterness for this life. She had no doubt that Morgan Tanner loved his son and that the mistakes he had made as a father were a result of simple ignorance and his own emotional turmoil over the loss of his wife. To her way of thinking, Morgan was as much a victim of the situation as Nolan himself, but she understood Morgan's need to somehow make amends.

Having already lost Nolan, she could find no justification whatever for banishing his father from their lives, especially when he was so terribly lonely. So it was that Morgan became a frequent visitor to the Vickers household, despite the distance of travel involved. Mary Judith soon came to look forward to his company, especially as Christmas approached, for he was inordinately solicitous and respectful of her feelings, and she doubted very much that she could have faced holidays alone with her daughter.

That was one thing she wouldn't have to do, though. Morgan was there when they decorated their tree, and he took such obvious delight in the proceedings that it was difficult to feel very sad. He came back the next evening with a trunk load of presents to put under the tree, and though Mary Judith scolded him she was delighted to see that Laine was thrilled by the bounty.

The child had been somewhat subdued of late, despite her declarations about not missing Nolan, and though Morgan was intent upon winning Laine's heart, she had been slow to respond, which was not like her at all. However, soon after that display of largess, the like of which Laine had never before experienced, the two of them became great friends, and Mary Judith was relieved to find that Laine's growing fondness for Morgan was not based on his ability to buy presents. In a short while it seemed to her that Morgan came primarily to romp and play with Laine, and that Laine considered him her best friend.

Mary Judith would sit and pretend to read or crochet while the two of them pushed toy cars around the living-room floor or played some simple card game. Morgan was a fantastic loser and before long he had Laine believing she was the greatest natural card shark or race-car driver ever born. It was a joy to watch them together, and yet it was agony, too, because it should have been Nolan down there on his knees sputtering like an automobile engine with a Texas drawl. That was the great pity and the fact of it, and nothing or no one could change it. But in spite of her great sadness, she would not have been any happier knowing how miserably Nolan had it.

For Nolan the situation could not have been more bleak, but by sheer dent of will he kept going like gangbusters over those next few weeks. He had chosen to move into an apartment in a building still under renovation by his fledgling company. It was to be a temporary arrangement. He was the first and only tenant, and though the lack of distractions allowed him to concentrate more completely than ever before on his work, the loneliness was almost more than he could bear. Consequently he worked even harder.

The results were amazing, even to himself. It seemed impossible for one man to accomplish so much in such a short period of time. Contracts for new projects were flowing in at an astounding rate, many of them in communities surrounding Denton. He was hiring new employees almost daily, and an established local developer with impeccable credentials had offered him a partnership. Boyd Carter was busy exploring the possibilities for his driven friend and attepting to hammer out an ironclad contract guaranteeing that history would not, could not, repeat itself. But still Nolan was not satisfied.

Something was missing in his life, had always been missing in his life, and though he blamed his father for that circumstance and told himself that his involvement with Mary Judith had been a mistake, he could not quell the mysterious ache that opened within him at every unguarded moment. He did not truly think much about Morgan. He'd had much too much practice at putting such thoughts out of his mind. But a certain vision of a woman and her child never actually left him, no matter how he worked to dispel it, and he woke one night from a dream of loving arms frantically reaching out to hold him to the conclusion that he had to do something to give himself peace or go stark raving mad.

The idea, that *something*, first began to take shape in his mind as he walked through the busy lobby of a local bank on his way to a meeting with its senior officers. There was an unusual bustle in the movement of the crowd that day, a feeling of lightheartedness despite the cold, gray blustery day, and he found himself stopping to take stock of those around him. There in the midst of a long winding line in front of the tellers' cages was a familiar face. Marta stood with her gaze trained steadily upon him, her face expressionless except for the slight curl of a smile at one corner of her mouth. He walked toward her, feeling suddenly dapper in the long overcoat and three-piece suit he seemed to be wearing with increasing frequency these days. She nodded as he approached.

"Nolan."

"Marta, it's good to see you again," he rattled off conversationally. "How have you been? Still at the old place? I suppose it's the same as ever."

She listened to his pathetic attempts at small talk without so much as a blink, then folded her hands and made a studied, patient reply. "No one else has moved out, if that's what you mean, and no one else has moved in."

"Oh." He'd sent a full month's rent in the mail, but Mary Judith had sent it back to him without comment, and he'd used that returned check to convince himself that his moving out had caused no financial hardship for her and Laine. The news that she'd not yet found another boarder was somewhat disturbing to an already burdened conscience. "I'm sorry," he mumbled, adding something about the new school term coming up soon; this meant to convey that there would be a turnover in tenancy and the vacancy at the boardinghouse was bound to be filled then.

Marta turned her gaze to the teller's window ahead. "You know, Nolan, you chose a particularly difficult time to cut out. It is Christmas, and every extra cent is appreciated at this time of year, especially when you're buying for a child."

He wondered if the grin on her face was prompted by the sudden paling of his. He dug his hands into his coat pockets, cleared his throat and attempted to change the subject.

"Is that what you're doing here," he asked brightly, "bracing the old pocketbook for the Yuletide buying season?"

She nodded. "Something like that." Then she impaled him with eyes that seemed to cut right through him. "Wouldn't hurt you to indulge in a little gift giving this season. You know what they say, 'tis better to give than to receive."

He shrugged his shoulders then and dropped his gaze to the floor. "Yeah, but it's the receiving part that worries me." He looked up and inquired softly, "Do you think she'd accept anything from me now?"

Marta hunched her shoulders noncommittally, but her eyes offered frank reassurance. "I think she'd take anything you offered her." He nodded gratefully and started away, but she caught him by the arm, adding, "Just be certain what it is you're willing to give this time, Nolan, because Mary Judith has friends who won't take it kindly if she's misled in any way."

"Yes," he said thickly, and gently disengaged her hand. "I can see that." He wished her a merry Christmas and went quickly on his way, convinced that he should stay as far from Mary Judith as possible for both their sakes. It was a frail conviction, however, without the strength to maintain itself in the face of that constant, haunting vision, and as the day of giving drew nearer, he found himself drawn more and more to the idea of making peace for friendship's sake. He wouldn't allow himself to stop and think that friendship with Mary Judith was about as possible as a daily commute to the sun and back, and by the time he made the firm decision to go ahead with this peace-finding mission of his, he'd quite satisfied himself that he had taken to heart the most important part of Marta's advice.

"Just be certain what it is you're willing to give this time, Nolan," she had said to him, and his reply was that he knew exactly what he was offering. Friendship, and nothing but. With a round-trip ticket to the sun.

Chapter Nine

Nolan came home to his new and roomy apartment every evening and was hit by the forlornness of it. Even the work was not enough to cushion him from the loneliness, and he began to find additional excuses to stay away. Marta had opened an excellent avenue of escape for him with her talk about giving. Having convinced himself that it was possible to be friends with Mary Judith, he set about arming himself with "peace offerings."

Once he'd actually begun shopping, the project seemed to balloon. His list got longer and longer and he found himself making long, extended forays into the malls and department stores, choosing gifts with the utmost care. Some were for old friends, some for new. A few went to distant relatives. Others he bought for mere acquaintances. He even went so far as to buy small articles for his former housemates, Gilly, Trish and, of course, Marta. After that it felt quite natural to choose gifts for Mary Judith and Laine. For Mary Judith he chose an elaborately carved pink alabaster jewelry box overlaid with white roses. After much agonizing he opted for an expensive version of a popular doll for Laine, and then as an afterthought picked up a read-aloud storybook.

He enjoyed the shopping and choosing immensely, which surprised and rather amused him, but the gift-giving process involved more than the buying. The gifts had to be delivered, and this was the sticky part. Oh, he had no difficulty presenting pen sets and brass card cases and monogrammed handkerchiefs to employees and business acquaintances, and it was no chore at all to send a variety of packages off in the mail. But then there were those half-dozen packages in their store wrappings waiting to be delivered, and he just couldn't seem to find a convenient time for that particular excursion. There they sat, evening after evening, daring him, until finally, a couple of days before Christmas, he couldn't stand to look at them anymore.

The weather was very un-Christmasy, even for Texas. It was as if an errant tropical breeze had settled over the area, and an overcast sky did nothing to dispel the balmy, tepid temperatures. Somehow Nolan found the unseasonable warmth depressing, and he could not help thinking of that first day when he'd driven his sports car up to this very sidewalk and stared through the window at the dignified but sagging old house. That day he'd wondered how he could possibly have come to this. Now he wondered why he couldn't leave it behind.

Just as before, he got out of the car, raised the trunk lid and lifted out a large cumbersome box, this one filled with various presents in colorful wrappings. He walked up the concrete path toward the porch behind the stately columns, and as he drew near he heard the shrill, high-pitched laughter of a tiny angel-faced girl. An ache erupted in him, like the sudden, sharp pricking of a missile; but at the same time, his heart seemed to lift in his chest, as if it literally jumped for joy. Then came the roar, a deep, angry growl that built into a threatening shout. First the laughter, then a pause like the intake of a breath and then that roar, full of anger and warning.

Nolan halted at the first step, his even, slightly jutting black brows drawn together in a deep crease, his ears cocked for more revealing noises. It was then that he caught the movement behind the glass-paneled door and trained his eyes on the small fuzzy figure at its etched top. The figure bounced and threw itself upward, then dropped immediately into view behind the clear portion of the glass. It was Laine, riding the banister in a crazy downward slide. He shook his head, a dizzying feeling of déjà vu engulfing him. Brave as a lion tamer, that kid. His chest swelled with pride as he watched the tiny figure plop onto the floor on her backside. The drop gave her quite a jolt. She lay there a moment before struggling up on her elbows.

It was then that he saw the feet, heavy feet, pounding down the stairs in those buff-colored suede shoes, Gilly's feet. Laine was up in a flash and racing across the foyer, with Gilly pounding the floorboards behind her, obviously in pursuit. Nolan wondered if the man had ever moved that fast before, but he didn't have time to dwell on the notion as Laine tore out the door and across the porch toward him, Gilly almost on top of her. Suddenly the big man reached out with both arms and swept her up in a bear hug. In that same moment Laine's eyes widened as she spotted Nolan.

Gilly stumbled to a halt, turned the child in his arms and began to shake her roughly, her dark head snapping back and forth as the ponytail flopped behind. Instinctively Nolan dropped the box and vaulted the steps in one fluid motion. He brought his arm down hard between them, over both of Gilly's, and the shaking instantly stopped. It was then that Nolan first noticed the blobs of white foam on Gilly's chin and chest and the sticky brown stain spreading downward over the shirtfront covering his protruding belly.

"You brat!" Gilly bawled, anger contorting his heavy features and trembling in his puffy jowls. "You did that on purpose!"

"I didn't do nothing!" Laine screeched, and Gilly made as if to shake her again, stopped only by the pressure of Nolan's arm and the steely hand gripping the flaccid flesh of his upper arm.

"Let her go, Gilbert. Now!" The taut, squarish jaw set determinedly. The finely wrought mouth pressed into a thin, authoritative line, brooking no challenge, accepting nothing less than full compliance.

Reluctantly Gilly loosened his hold on the girl and she slid to the floor. Whereupon she sent a well-aimed toe at Gilly's shin and they were off again, Gilly roaring like a bull elephant as he brushed off an unprepared Nolan and charged after the child. Her flight was a short one. He caught her as she descended the porch steps and had her across his knees before Nolan could turn and breach the distance between them. Laine squirmed like an earthworm on hot cement. Gilly whacked her a glancing blow on the seat of the pants, and she yelped, more in outrage than pain. Gilly lifted his hand, but Nolan dropped onto the ground at his side and gripped the thick wrist, halting it in midair.

Gilly's eyes came up and locked with Nolan's. For a brief moment his arm strained against Nolan's hold, and the dark-brown eyes widened in surprise at the fat man's strength. Then something like defeat trembled about the full, glum mouth, and the straining arm relaxed. It was then—when the fight had gone out of her opponent and rescue was assured—that Laine began to wail. Nolan looked at her as if she were a rare species of life, while Gilly focused on his shirtfront.

"Scream, you brat!" he bawled at her. "I'd scream, too, if I was an ill-mannered, spoiled-rotten little troublemaker!"

Nolan shook him, and Laine rolled off his lap, landing with a slap of palms on the edge of the lower step. She screamed with fresh vigor, and Nolan shot her a concerned look. "Are you all right?" For a response, she screamed louder but seemed unhurt, at which point he turned back to Gilly for answers. A tiny glob of white that Nolan could now identify as a piece of melted marshmallow clung to a button straining at the edge of a ragged buttonhole.

"My Christmas cocoa," the big man sulked, his gaze trained on the dark stain plunging over the rise of his belly. "I offered her a cup and she poured it on me!"

Laine leaped up then and began to scream at him, "Liar! Liar!" Nolan spun around and grasped her by the shoulders, shaking her.

"Stop that!" he commanded, thoroughly confused by her behavior. She seemed to catch her breath and really look at him for the first time, then her tiny face screwed up and suddenly she was lashing out at him, her fists and feet flying in hysterical rage.

"I hate you! I hate you!" she screamed, and with horror Nolan realized that she meant him. He released her abruptly, oblivious to Mary Judith's arrival. The child tore up the steps past Gilly to the opened doorway, where her mother stood, trying to take in the scene. Weeping loudly, Laine threw herself at Mary Judith's trousered legs. Mary Judith embraced her daughter, her gaze trained on Nolan, who turned dazedly to stare at the mother and child.

"Nolan." She acknowledged him in a low tremulous voice, then turned her attention fully to the weeping child. Nolan turned away and began self-consciously to gather the scattered presents, paying little attention to the flattened bows and nicked foil wrappings.

Mary Judith spoke quietly to Laine, whose sobbings had subsided somewhat, then sent her inside and focused her attention on Gilly, who stood before her with his head hanging like that of a disobedient, overgrown boy. "What's this about?" she demanded evenly, and he began an anxious explanation of how he had offered Laine a cup of his special Christmas cocoa, only to have the cup knocked out of his hand and the contents spilled over his front. There was no doubt that it had been intentional, and she had turned at once and fled. Naturally he had chased after her, but before he could administer the spanking she so obviously needed, Nolan had intervened.

As he told his story he grew bolder, and it was apparent that he was building to a rousing commentary on Laine's misdeeds and her need for discipline, but Mary Judith allowed him no opportunity. As soon as she'd had the whole story, she interrupted his discourse firmly.

"Thank you, Gilly. I'm sorry this happened, and I assure you I'll deal with it. Now I think you'd best go and change. Drop those clothes in some cold water until I come up for them. I think we'll let Laine wash them by hand. That should teach her a lesson."

He seemed less than completely pleased with the pronounced punishment but anxious to be away now that Mary Judith's attention had turned pointedly to Nolan. He took himself off, muttering about all the things wrong with the world, chief among them being mischievous children.

Nolan held his box of offerings before him like a buffer and slowly climbed the steps, his feet making scraping sounds. "How are you?" he asked, appalled at the husky, whispery quality of his voice. She wrapped her arms tightly about her middle, her stance defensive, wary. She seemed almost frightened of him, and that caused a roiling in his stomach and a sharp acidic taste to develop in his mouth. He looked away and swallowed the bitter lump in his throat.

"I think you just got a firsthand view of how I am, Nolan," she answered testily. "My longest resident boarder is about ready to pull out on me at a time when I already have not one but two empty apartments, and my normally well-behaved daughter seems to be living in a constant stage of upheaval and revolt. I'm at my wit's end with her and Gilly both, and what in heaven's name do you think you're doing?"

Her gaze riveted to the box in his arms and the colored shapes poking up beyond its rim.

He glanced down into the box and felt his face mottle with color. "I, um, I'm trying to make amends," he said, and thought of Laine and her remembered screams. The pain of that shot through him, and he squeezed his eyes shut. Suddenly he knew he couldn't bear for that child to hate him. He lifted his gaze abruptly. "Can I talk to her?" he asked, knowing Mary Judith understood.

"And explain what, Nolan? Why you abandoned her?"

He shook his head, the muscles of his jaws contracting from the bitter taste rising again in his mouth. "No. I want her to understand that I *haven't* abandoned her—or you." She tossed him an incredulous look, her chin lifting in disbelief. "Judith, you know I was...reluctant...to become involved with you. But it was because I knew what kind of job I had ahead of me and that the time was all wrong for romantic involvements." He noticed the sudden intake of her breath and hurried on, struggling for the words. "Nevertheless, I do care about you."

"So you said," she replied cryptically. He ignored her, his back going rigid, his eyes wide with determination.

"The three of us care about each other!" he declared doggedly. "We ought to be friends. You said that yourself once, more or less. My mistake was in letting it go beyond that. I knew better. I just..."

"Couldn't help yourself?" she put in cattily. "That makes it all right, does it? Stop and think about that a moment, will you? You say we never should have been more than friends, but that you just couldn't stop it from becoming more than that. I suppose that makes some sort of sense to you. *And* I suppose you're going to say that you couldn't stop yourself from walking out of here in a huff, either, because I happen to have been civil to a person who loves you very much, a person you have treated as unfairly as you've treated me and my daughter!'' She was shouting at him, and he felt a predictable surge of anger. Frustration was crowding up in him.

"You know it's a toss-up, lady, as to who has been unfair to whom! My father may seem like a poor defenseless old man to you, but I know better! You want to hear about poor and defenseless? Let me tell you about a poor defenseless kid who lost the only parent who ever really cared about him. You know, other people have lost loved ones besides you, and at least you had Laine after your husband died! I had nothing, no one. My father didn't care a whit about me. Maybe he says he did, but he didn't!''

He was shaking so badly he felt the box bumping around in his arms and tightened his hold on it. He closed his eyes and tried to get a firmer grip on himself, too. He couldn't go on talking about this. Whenever he tried to talk about this, he always had this same feeling, as if everything was slipping away from him, as if he was losing control. He pulled in a deep breath and forced himself to calm down.

"You can't understand what it was like," he said tightly. "I woke up every day of my life knowing I was nothing more than an inconvenience and a disappointment to him.'' She started to speak then, but he cut her off by turning his head sharply. He couldn't bear the look of pity in her eyes. It was not pity he wanted. It was—what? Understanding? How could he hope to make her understand what he himself found so confusing? He remembered the many times he had lain facedown on his bed and wept, ashamed to let his father hear. His father had never wept when his mother had died, not once, ever. Was Laine weeping now and feeling ashamed, as he had done for his own outbursts of uncontrollable rage and pain? He wanted suddenly to run to her and hold her until the weeping stopped. "Please," he said through clenched teeth, "let's not have another of these useless arguments. Just let me try to talk to Laine. I think I can help."

Mary Judith stared at him for a moment, then dropped her head and stepped aside. Nolan brushed past her and hurried across the foyer and into the apartment. He looked around, then walked briskly to the kitchen and stuck his head inside. Finding it empty, he started down the hall, the box of gifts held tightly in his arms.

Laine lay on the edge of her bed, staring up at the pink, ruffly canopy overhead. She didn't look at him, but she knew he was there.

"Laine?"

She rolled over onto her side, effectively turning her back to him. "Go away," she muttered. "I don't want to talk to you."

Nolan's mind was racing, searching for the best way to deal with her, but he appeared calm and very sure of himself as he strolled across the narrow room to stand beside the bed. "All right," he said, "you don't have to talk to me. But I want to talk to you." He looked down at the box in his arms and then at the huddled form of the child. "I brought some Christmas gifts," he said, dumping the contents of the box beside her on the bed.

"I don't want 'em."

"Well, that's up to you, too, but then they're not all yours." He bent over and tossed one of the packages off by itself. "This one's for Trish. Want to know what it is?" She made no response, but he went on, anyway. "It's one of those little folding mirrors that you keep in your purse. You know, you open it up and a little light comes on. That way she can practice in private."

"Practice?" Laine reached out and timidly fingered the slightly lopsided bow clinging to the small package. Nolan leaned forward until he'd brought his face into her view. She glanced up at him. "Practice what?" Her tone was glum, but Nolan thought he detected a glimmer of genuine interest, and for reply he batted his eyelashes furiously. Laine quickly looked away, but a smile tickled at her mouth. Nolan seized the opportunity.

"And guess what's in this one," he said, plopping onto the foot of the bed and reaching for a flat rectangular package. Laine said nothing, but she took the package from his hand when he offered it. "They're handkerchiefs. Great big ones. Big as bedsheets!"

She turned the package over in her hand, frowning. "Who're they for?"

He waited until she looked up, then pretended to carefully unfold something, shake it out, tuck it beneath his chin and smooth it over a rotund belly. Laine began to laugh.

"Ho, boy!" she said, scrambling up to sit cross-legged at the head of the bed. "That's Gilly, for sure." She sobered a bit and looked over at him guiltily. "Guess I'm in trouble, huh?"

He shrugged. "Could be worse, but I don't think that's what really matters, is it?" She slowly shook her head, frowning, and he reached across to clamp a hand over hers, commanding her attention. "Why'd you do it, honey?" She sat very still for a moment, then her bottom lip began to quiver. It struck him how much like her mother she was, and again he wanted to reach out and hug her, but he feared it would be premature on his part. "Laine? Want to tell me what happened?"

"I don't know!" she suddenly shrieked. "He said I was a pain in the neck and he'd give me a cup of cocoa if I'd go away, but I didn't want his old cocoa! I'm glad I spilled it! I don't like him anyway! He's not my friend! He's not my friend!"

Nolan quickly gathered her into his arms and began to rock gently back and forth. "That's okay, baby. Don't cry now. Gilly was wrong to say those things to you. You're not a pain in the neck. You're a sweet, wonderful little girl, and if he's just too silly to realize that, well, that's his problem." He kept rocking and talking and the child settled into his lap for a long cleansing weep. "You know, I kind of feel sorry for old Gilly. He's not a very nice person most of the time, and he doesn't seem to have any friends at all. Why, he can't even recognize a beautiful, sweet little person when he sees her. No wonder he's all alone and grouchy all the time. It must be awful not to have friends. I bet he wouldn't even know how to go about making a friend." He looked down at the tear-drenched face and saw eyes as big and round and gleaming as brand-new copper pennies.

"I'm not a very nice person sometimes," she whispered, and then she began to wail anew. "Oh, Nolan, I'm sorry! I didn't want you to go away!"

He squeezed her tighter. His throat felt soft and doughy. "Ah, sweetie, you didn't do anything to make me go away, and I didn't mean you to think I was going forever. I can't explain it, honey. It's all complicated, but it doesn't have anything to do with you. I'm sorry if you thought that, because you're just about my best little friend in the whole world! And listen, we're still going to see each other. I've got this big new apartment just a few blocks from here, and you can come over and visit me there, and we'll go places, too. We'll go to movies and to the park, and we'll go to the carnival when it comes to town. You'd like that, wouldn't you?"

She nodded eagerly, her cheek rubbing his shoulder. "Can we go tonight?" she snuffled.

"To the carnival? Well, gee, honey, I don't think there's one anywhere around here."

"There's an animated movie showing at the cinema on University," Mary Judith said, coming to lean in the doorway. She had obviously been listening to the entire conversation—and approved. He sent her a grateful look.

"How about it, pumpkin? Want to take in a movie with me?"

Laine sat up straight in his lap, a jubilant expression on her damp, lovely face. "Oh, swell!" She threw her arms around his neck and squeezed, then abruptly drew back, her face screwing up again. "Nolan, I didn't mean it. Honest, I didn't. I don't hate you!" He dried her eyes with his fingers.

"I know it," he said. "Listen, I understand. Sometimes, when you love somebody and they do something to hurt you, well, maybe it feels like you hate them, but you really don't. Now I'm going to make you a promise and then we'll just forget about this whole episode, okay?" He crooked a finger beneath her chin and spoke very purposefully. "I promise you I'll always be your friend, no matter what!"

She hugged him again and then he put her down and said she ought to get dressed, and that if it was okay with her mom they'd have a hamburger before the movie. Her troubles forgotten, Laine started pulling articles of clothing from drawers and trying to decide what to wear. Nolan and Mary Judith quietly left the room.

"I'm sorry," he said as soon as they'd entered the living room. "I guess I kind of threw her a loop when I left here the way I did. I should've realized how it might affect her, but it just never occurred to me that she would feel so strongly about it. Sometimes adults get the idea that kids don't feel things as strongly as they do, but I should've known better."

"Yes," Mary Judith said quietly. "You should have, since you remember your own childhood feelings so well. Tell me, Nolan, has it never occurred to you that your father might have made that mistake? You see how easy it is to jump to those kinds of conclusions? Maybe, in the beginning, after your mother died, he just didn't realize how you felt."

Nolan stared at her. Could it be? Almost reflexively he hardened his heart against the vision of his father foundering in a miasma of confused emotions and mistaken notions. He wouldn't feel sorry for the old man. How many years had Morgan had to do what he had just done, to correct his mistakes? He had shown Laine that he cared for her, that he understood her feelings. How could Morgan ever do the same? And even if he found the right words to say, how could he, Nolan, ever trust them after all the years of animosity, all the arguments, all the criticism. He shook his head.

"It isn't the same, Judith. You're still talking about something you know nothing about. I came here to make peace with you and to get us on the proper footing. I want to make it right, believe me."

She stared at him for the longest time, her head slowly shaking from side to side. "Don't you see, Nolan, it can never be right between us as long as we want different things. I want marriage and partnership and family. You want friendship. It isn't enough, Nolan. I'm sorry, it just isn't enough, not for me. And you might as well know now that the only reason I will let you come back into our lives is for Laine's sake. She needs you in a different way than I want you, but don't expect me to be glad. Don't expect me to be happy. Don't expect me to understand, because I can't. Some part of me will always believe that we should have been together."

He felt the most awful tightening in his chest and loins. His arms wanted to open for her, to close around her, but he panicked, a chill fluttering up his spine, and he stayed them. He believed, he honestly believed, that he could not have this love and that elusive something toward which he drove himself. He could not be sidetracked. He could not be slowed. A course had been chosen for him, and he *had* to stick with it. It was not her course, and he couldn't expect her to travel it, never knowing what they were running toward, never understanding the distant goal.

He'd seen his parents try to live that kind of life. He'd seen his mother long for the attention of her husband, struggling to understand him. He'd seen his father distance himself from them, could still hear his mother explaining that daddy had to concentrate on his business, that successful men had to concentrate on business. He'd known she was ill long before his father had noticed. He'd listened to her apologize over and over again for the trouble she was causing, for the inconvenience of having to die slowly, and he'd heard his father's short, ineffectual replies and seen his mother smile up at him gratefully, as if he'd forgiven her a mighty sin. He wouldn't become the kind of man his father was. He wouldn't be that.

He looked down at his hands. "Judith," he told her hoarsely, "I'm doing what I think best." To his surprise, her reply came back soft and gentle.

"Yes," she said, and he lifted his gaze to find a reluctant smile curving her lips. "I'm sure you are. But when are you going to understand, darling, that Morgan, too, did what he thought best? He was wrong in many instances, but he tried to raise you the best way he knew how, and that ought to count for something."

Nolan wanted to say that Morgan's best was not good enough, but she murmured that she must help Laine dress and quickly exited, leaving him there with his quizzical, contradictory notions. The thing about Mary Judith, he told himself, was that she turned the world upside down and inside out, and he just didn't have time to be continually righting it. He just didn't have time.

Laine was a perfect angel. Nolan didn't know a kid could enjoy a movie so much or that an adult could enjoy a kid's enjoyment so much. He did experience a pang or two of regret early on in the evening when he remembered the blueprints clipped to his drawing board at the office, and he'd rushed dinner a bit so that he could make a couple of important phone calls before the movie, but Laine had seemed content to stand there holding his hand and smiling up at him while he'd explained to the foreman of the apartment-complex job on Avenue J why it would be necessary to send a subcontractor's crew temporarily to the office-building job on Scripture.

To his surprise, during the movie he didn't even think about what he could do to get that little remodeling job over on Carroll back onto schedule. Instead he found himself involved in the ludicrous, beautifully animated adventures of a pack of mice! He munched on Laine's popcorn and hooted at a goony bird and smiled to himself because they were having such fun. On the way home he let her fiddle with the stereo in his car, quite forgetting that it was a finely tuned instrument, and again smiled to himself as he watched from the corner of his eye how she enjoyed the music. He wondered at the difference in being six now and being six when he was six. Life was full of mysteries and odd joys. He ruminated on this subject until they reached home and then was surprised to find that his little companion had dropped off to sleep while he wasn't watching.

He went around the car, opened the door and carefully unbuckled her belt. She roused enough to put her arms about his neck while he gently lifted her from the seat. The night had gotten chilly and she had not zipped her coat up all the way, so he hugged her to his chest as he carried her up the walk, marveling at the look of utter relaxation on her face. He rang the buzzer with a well-placed knee and Mary Judith came quickly to hold the door.

Swiftly, quietly, he carried the sleeping child through the lighted foyer and into the darkened apartment. The TV was tuned in to the evening news, and yellow flames flickered in the fireplace, giving the room an intimate feel. A stocking hung on the mantel and a tall, full spruce stood in a dark corner near the window, its lights twinkling like colored stars. He hurried through, the warmth and gentle intimacy of the place a pleasure to him. Down the hallway and past the bathroom and Mary Judith's own room and then he had reached that frilly pink room, too frilly pink for an angel-faced tomboy, it seemed.

A nightlight in the shape of a strawberry glowed dimly in one corner. The covers were turned back and a fuzzy puppy dog with floppy ears but no nose and only a torn wisp of a red felt tongue lay next to the pillow. He deposited Laine gently beside the worn toy and began to carefully release the zipper of her coat and extract her thin arms from the sleeves. Mary Judith then stepped in to remove her shoes and the outer layers of her clothing before tucking the covers around the mute form that reached for the stuffed puppy and snuggled into place.

He watched, feeling fatherly and protective and as big as the room, her coat with the pocketed mittens still in his hand, while Mary Judith gently worked the rubber band from the sagging ponytail and spread the black curtain of hair over the pillow. She bent and kissed her daughter good-night, her hand soothing a brow not in the least furrowed, and he felt so much a part of it that a new and powerful conviction filled him. This would work. He could fulfill an important part of this child's life. He could be here for her, and this friendship could be real and satisfying. What she needed, he could give, and his own life would be the better for it, not different, but better.

Then he followed Mary Judith as she tiptoed from the room and down the hall back to that cozy place where the fireplace danced with yellow light, and he smiled at her as she stood there, clutching the white-piped collar of her robe, her eyes heavy with the lateness of the hour, her face clean and dewy fresh, her hair tumbling and coiling in wild disarray, and suddenly he knew the fiercest surge of desire he'd ever felt, and the bottom dropped out of his conviction.

He stuffed his hands in his pockets and tried to ignore the tightening in his loins. He wanted to get out of there, and he wanted to stay, and he knew which one he was going to do, and he almost hated himself for it. But there was that path all laid out for him, and he too far down it to quit now. So he gritted his teeth and said something perfectly reasonable about the movie and how he'd better be going, and hoped with all his heart she'd beg him to stay, wouldn't *let* him leave, would hang her arms around his neck and plead for just one incredibly exquisite night until it would simply have to be. What she did was to invite him to spend Christmas with them, and then she made that impossible by telling him flatly that his father would be there and she would expect pleasant behavior at every turn. He declined and thanked her and walked

out, a feeling of betrayal coming up hard against his
desire, that rock-solid determination guiding his feet
and that emptiness already widening inside him.

Chapter Ten

Christmas was pleasant enough for Mary Judith, but for Laine it was excitingly different than in previous years. She bounded from bed on that morning to find her usual stocking filled with nuts and fruit and sweets and the usual reasonable array of carefully chosen toys and articles of clothing, but the enjoyment had only begun. Morgan showed up earlier than he had planned, and Laine at last got to tear into those tantalizing packages that had been stacked beneath the tree for so long. He was immensely pleased with his choices and in her reactions to them, and Mary Judith was delighted to see both of them having such fun, but she could not help thinking of Nolan.

Was he alone or with friends of whom she knew nothing? She hoped he was not alone. She genuinely hoped he was not alone, but she felt certain that he was. While Morgan and Laine turned her living room into playland, she slipped away under the guise of tending her Christmas dinner and used the phone in the kitchen to call information for Nolan's number. For some reason she'd expected difficulty getting it, but the operator rattled off the seven digits in bored tones, adding a slightly more enthusiastic "Merry Christmas" before ringing off. She dialed the number hesitantly and was further surprised when Nolan promptly answered.

"Tanner," he said, and she felt a certain amount of relief at the cheery tone.

"Merry Christmas."

"Judith! Merry Christmas! How's the munchkin taking it?"

"She's having a ball. Morgan's in there playing with her now. Ever seen a grown man cooing to a pug-faced doll? She loves it, by the way. We've named her Bonnie."

A slight pause, then a hearty, "Bonnie! Well, well, that's a great name. Glad she's pleased."

"She'd be happier if you'd come over for dinner."

"I told Boyd Carter I'd be at his place for dinner. Maybe I could drop by later. She going to be busy around five?"

"We're attending vesper service."

"Oh?"

"The three of us."

"Oh."

"You're welcome to come along. It's really a lovely little chapel and the music is always so very..."

"Listen, I'm running a bit late here, so you guys have a good one and tell Laine I'll drop by in the middle of the week—unless you'd rather I didn't."

"No, that will be fine."

"Great. See you."

"Nolan?"

"Yeah?"

"I know where you got it. He's wonderful with her, just the way you are. Isn't that strange, Nolan? I mean, isn't that ironic?"

She sensed the lightheartedness slip out of his mood, then felt the silence hardening at the end of the line.

"He's really made himself a part of the family, hasn't he?" he commented bitterly. "Well, I won't pretend I'm not surprised. Apparently you've seen a side of him I was never privileged to see. I just hope he never shows you the side I got."

She gripped the phone. Her heart felt as if it weighed about a hundred pounds. "I didn't mean it to work out this way, Nolan," she told him softly. "You were the one I wanted. You still are."

"Judith," he said in a sad whisper, and then he hung up.

She put the phone receiver back on the hook and stood there with the sounds and smells of Christmas floating around her, wondering if this love was wrong, as he claimed. She thought of Mick and of the trauma of losing him, and she knew beyond any doubt that that love had been no mistake. She thought of Nolan and the times he had taken her in his arms and the way he had touched her to the very soul. If she had allowed him to make love to her that night, would it be different now? Would he be with her, inescapably bound? Would he be happy? Would she? She thought of his chiseled features, the sleek black hair she had always favored, the long strong arms, the hands that had so gently eased the coat from Laine's sleeping body. She thought of certain moments the three of them had spent together, the ease of those times, the unguarded naturalness, and she thought of how he drew into himself at the mention of his father's name, how he tried to distance himself from them and yet could not quite escape. The mistake was not hers. It was little comfort, but at least she knew the mistake was not hers.

Nolan made himself stay away two extra days. He thought it would be easy, at first, for Christmas had been deceptively restful. He had rattled around the apartment for a while, expecting to feel the old loneliness engulf him, but the place had seemed almost livable for a change, and he had found the solitude to be relaxing, for once. Not even Mary Judith's phone call had significantly interrupted the tranquility of the day. He had simply put it out of his mind. Why shouldn't he? They had seemed as reasonably content as he. It was just the picture of his father romping around with Laine that wouldn't go away.

He couldn't for the life of him quite believe it. Morgan Tanner was a tough old nut, and no one knew that better than him. Nolan had seen him with kids before. Once, he remembered, Boyd's oldest boy had crawled up in Morgan's lap and sat there smiling. Morgan had smiled back, but stiffly, and gone on talking as if the kid was not sitting there begging for attention with his eyes. After a bit the boy had gotten down and toddled off. Morgan had stretched his neck and tugged at his tie, obviously relieved. But Boyd's kid was not Laine. He supposed that if any kid could crack the shell of that tough old nut, Laine Vickers was the one. But why should that make him feel proud, as if he'd had something to do with it when he knew he hadn't?

Boyd's wife had made a good meal. Camden was there, asking nosy questions and dropping juicy tidbits, but they all generally ignored him, and the day passed pleasantly enough. Boyd's kids—he had three of them now, all boys—were busy with their various presents. One of them was an expensive stereo unit that the oldest kept blaring until Boyd marched upstairs and pulled the plug. Nolan had to shake his head. Kids do grow up. He didn't even look like the same boy who had crawled onto Morgan's lap. Had it really been that long ago? No matter. Morgan couldn't have changed so much. Or could he? It was then that he'd decided not to go around to Mary Judith for at least a couple of days. Just a certain sound in that woman's voice could put the strangest thoughts in his head.

By the next morning, however, the apartment had somehow reverted back to that empty, cell-like place he'd always felt it to be, and he couldn't wait to get out and about. Unfortunately there was no place more welcoming to go. The office was empty and dark. The secretary and bookkeeper he'd hired wouldn't be back to work for two more days. Because it was the end of the year and the dual holidays of Christmas and New Year's fell on weekdays, the work week would be short. No one was doing much anyway. Construction always slowed down at this time of year. People almost invariably put off making major decisions until January. He really didn't have anything pressing to attend. He added a few finishing touches to some plans he had been drawing and then put them away neatly. The client wouldn't be coming in to look at them for days and days.

After that he went back to the apartment and did a whole series of calisthenics and aerobic exercises. He did them again the next morning and again that afternoon. That night he went out and bought himself a new television and a video recorder to go with it. The temperature outside dropped about thirty degrees during the hour or so he was in the store, and sometime later it began to sleet. He got up that next morning and went out to get the newspaper. It was encrusted in ice.

It wasn't so bad, though. It was cold, to be sure, but the sun was out and the sky was a light clear blue. He wondered if Laine had ever been ice skating and if the roads would be clear enough to drive her into Dallas to one of the big rinks. He dressed in black slacks and a black ribbed turtleneck and dug out his heavy, fleece-lined suede coat.

The car didn't want to start, but he coaxed it a little and soon he was creeping along nearly deserted streets. He circled around Mary Judith's block because the street in front of her house was a one-way street and he didn't want to make any sharp turns getting to it. The ice wasn't all that bad, but any kind of ice in Texas was trouble because most parts just didn't get enough of it for the public to get educated about how to drive on the stuff. He noticed several city police cars out and about, prepared to work a bevy of accidents once things got moving. He saluted one guy as he drove by and the officer gave him a quizzical look, as if wondering what he had to be so happy about on this cold, icy winter morning. Nolan didn't know why himself, but he just felt good, clean.

He pulled up in front of Mary Judith's house, missing his regular spot by a few feet as the car slid a little farther than it usually did after he applied the brakes. He looked up and a bundled and capped Laine was sliding down the gentle slope of the walk toward him, her mother coming along behind at a more careful pace. They were laughing and their breaths froze on the air like little clouds of pixie dust, and he felt really good then, as if he'd awaken from a dark and murky dream to the brilliant light of day. He got out and caught her in a bear hug as she slid up on the soles of her shoes.

"I'm skating! I'm skating!" she exclaimed.

"You sure are! Just be careful and don't bruise that little tush."

"What's a tush?"

"Never mind," Mary Judith intervened neatly, and he let her go. She slipped along, her arms flailing to maintain balance, then tumbled over into the grass. She giggled wildly and was up again before he had time to get concerned. Mary Judith turned to him with a playfully censorious smile. "You, teaching my kid words like tush!"

"Well, what'd you want me to say?"

"How about 'bottom'?"

He rolled his eyes, teasing her. "Jars have bottoms. Boxes have bottoms. Holes in the ground have bottoms. People have tushes."

"People have heads, too, and I'm going to conk you on yours if you don't watch your language."

She shook a fist at him and the action rocked her balance enough to send her feet flying out from beneath her. He caught her against him, and they both fell back against the fender of the car, which supported them. He laughed and almost kissed her before he remembered. Then the awkwardness had them and the laughter felt tight and stilted.

"We'd better move off this slick sidewalk before someone gets hurt." She called to Laine, and then they both started across the yard, the yellowish grass crunching beneath their feet. Halfway to the porch, they stopped to wait for the child to catch up. She ran toward them, crunch, crunch, crunch.

"Don't go in!" she pleaded. "Let's stay out a little longer."

Judith gave her permission, and Nolan caught the child's hand. Soon they were breaking icicles from the eaves of the house and punching them into the grass to make designs on the lawn. They had been out only a few minutes when the sound of a car being driven with tire chains caught his attention, and he looked up to see the long black limousine that belonged to his father pulling up next to the sidewalk. Laine raised a hand to shield her eyes and get a better look. Mary Judith, too, stared, and he knew from her expression that she had not seen the limo before. Nolan tugged at his gloves as his father stepped carefully from the back seat. Laine clapped her hands together when she saw who it was, and Nolan felt his face begin to burn with jealousy.

"I've got to go," he muttered, but the child turned a face full of disappointment up at him.

"But you just got here!" she whined.

He flashed a look at Mary Judith, the crunching sound of his father's footsteps growing louder and more ominous. She, too, had that pleading look on her face and a sadness that said she couldn't ask Morgan to leave. Anger flashed up in him, constricted his throat. It was unfair, damned unfair!

A hand descended on his shoulder then, and he knew from the feel of it that it was his father's, yet it was curiously light and fragile. He looked down at it, and it looked like none he had ever seen before. His father's hand was strong and firm and hard, like his own.

"I'm glad you're here, son," said his father softly. "I've been hoping to see you, to talk to you."

Nolan shook his head. That was not his father's voice. It was older and thinner and it didn't have that edge of sharpness to it. "I can't stay," he said brusquely, and shrugged off the hand. He started across the grass, his head down, his feet stomping the ice casings to shards.

"Nolan!" his father called, and then came the sounds of him following. "Nolan!" he said, stopping short of the sidewalk as the younger man stepped gingerly across it and reached the car. "Wait!" he demanded. "Are you so afraid of me that you can't just listen for once?" Nolan drew up, his hand reaching toward the door handle, and slowly turned.

"I stopped being afraid of you twenty years ago," he shouted, "when I got big enough to knock you down!"

The old man closed his eyes. So old he seemed in that harsh daylight that Nolan could scarcely believe it was him. The skin on his face was papery and thin, still taut, but thin, with the blue veins beneath showing through. That shock of white at his forehead seemed to have grown wider, whiter, and to have spread thinly throughout the once black hair. Immaculately dressed in a tailored coat, he seemed thin and wasted. Old. He was old.

"I was a poor excuse for a father," he said, his voice trembling with more emotion than Nolan could ever remember hearing from him. "But I am so very proud of the man you turned out to be. I love you. There. What I've wanted to say all these many years. I love you. And she loves you." He jerked his head at Mary Judith, who was moving cautiously down the walk toward them.

Nolan stared at him. All these many years, he thought, too many, too damned many! He said nothing, for there was nothing to be said, as strange as that seemed, even to him. He reached for the handle of the car door, pulled it, swung the door open.

"Stop," Morgan pleaded. "Stop and think, Nolan, what you're doing, what you're becoming. Don't let yourself become the thing you've hated the most. Don't be like me, measuring yourself only by the profit-and-loss columns of all those senseless deals!"

Like him, Nolan thought. No! Never! I won't let my life become like his. I won't make the mistake of trying to have everything my way. He should never have married my mother. But then, he thought, wouldn't that have made him like me?

There was an answer there somewhere, but with all this stuff going around inside of him, all this resentment and anger and hatred. *"Sometimes,"* he'd said to Laine, "when you love somebody and they do something to hurt you, it feels like you hate them. But you don't." Oh, God, he had to get away from there. Why had he come? Every time he came, things always got so jumbled up.

Mary Judith got there and stood with her hands clamped tightly together, those big green eyes wide with hope. "Oh, Nolan," she said, "please stay. I want you to stay." But he couldn't, not now.

"I'll call you later," he mumbled, and ducked down into the car.

"No!" she said, bending low to see his face. "It's now or never, Nolan. We love you. All three of us love you! And you love us, too, but you're so damned afraid of it you just won't let it be!"

"You've never understood!" he accused. "You've never understood that I have to do something, I have to make this business work, and I won't do it at the expense of people I care about!"

"But you are!" Morgan insisted. "Can't you see that you already are. And it doesn't have to be that way, Nolan. I learned that when your mother was dying. Don't you remember how I stayed by her through that time? How I tended her myself? It surprised me, but the company didn't go down the tubes. It didn't fall apart. Business slacked off a bit, but there was plenty of money coming in, and for what? The money never meant anything. Haven't you figured that out yet? The money's the least of it!"

Nolan stared at his father through the doorway of the car. "I remember how she apologized for taking you away from the business," he uttered bitterly.

His father nodded, sighed. "Yes. I never knew how to respond to that. I never knew what to say. That was my problem, Nolan. I never knew how to say what was in my heart, but then I didn't have to say it with your mother. She knew. She always knew. I guess I just expected you to know, too." His hands, too pale, too thin, too fragile, lifted and fell at his sides in a gesture of impotence, and suddenly Nolan wanted to believe it was that simple.

But how could it be? All these years of estrangement, all this time of hurting and struggling against it. It couldn't have been so simple that a few words could have made the difference. *"I love you,"* this old man had said, and Nolan thought of all the times he would have rejoiced to hear his father say that! But wasn't it too late? This old man, how could he be the father he had hated all these years? Nolan slammed the door and started the engine. He checked the street automatically, but he didn't see the trio of cars creeping slowly along, didn't see the familiar black-and-white sedan riding herd on the others.

The car swung away from the curb in a wider arc than he had intended, and he brought it deftly back into line, glancing in the side-view mirror, checking, just checking. They were standing there on the lawn watching and getting smaller, that fragile-looking old man and that wonderful little kid, and that woman who could turn his world upside down by just wanting him. Just wanting him! It struck him then. They were his family. That old man might be the only one related to him, but as surely as the sun set in the west they were his family. And saying it wasn't so didn't change things. But what to do? How to know what was best?

"Now or never," Mary Judith had said. Right now, right at this moment, she loved him. She loved him like no other person on the face of the earth ever had—right now. What if no one ever loved him like that again? *"Now or never."* Never was a damned long time to spend making money he didn't really need anyway! Morgan was right about that much, at least.

The money was the least of it, the very, very least of it. And if Morgan was right about that, what else was he right about, and how much courage did a man have to have to admit he was wrong?

Suddenly he knew he was the biggest fool who had ever lived. Everyone who loved him, everything he loved, every dream he'd ever had, every wish he'd ever made was standing back there on that lawn growing smaller and dimmer with each passing second, and the only thing that prevented him from turning around was that monstrous Tanner pride! Well, not quite, there was a sign just about where he stopped that said ONE WAY in big, bold letters, and the street was far too slick to turn around. So he slammed it into reverse and there he was weaving and sliding backward when the lights started flashing and cars started skidding every which direction, and he realized with a laugh that he'd messed it up real good this time. But not too bad. Maybe. If he hurried.

Mary Judith was watching when he put on the brakes and slid to a screeching, smoking halt, and her heart jumped up in her throat right about then, thumping to beat the band and sending waves of hope and exultation and jubilation through her. Then she saw the car start backing up and covered her eyes, a scream stuck in her throat, trying to get past her heart. The screeching and the roaring stopped with a kind of anticlimactic *thunk*, and Morgan exclaimed something low and relieved sounding under his breath. Laine was hooting, and Judith became dimly aware of Laine's running past her as she lowered her hands.

It was chaos. There was a cop shouting at Nolan, who was trying to pull away, and a man in jeans and corduroy coat was trying to get out of his car but his feet kept slipping out from under him on the icy street. Another man and a woman were standing in the grass on the opposite side of the street, looking at the front end of their car, which had jumped the curb but didn't appear to be damaged. None of that mattered, though, because Nolan had extricated himself from the policeman's grasp and was slowly backing toward them. He nodded continually and was talking a mile a minute, though she couldn't hear a word he was saying, and then the policeman pushed his hat back and scratched his head and busied himself with a black leather case he had taken from his hip pocket, and it was then that Nolan turned around and started running—or trying to.

Mary Judith gasped as his feet went off in different directions and he bent forward just in time to keep himself from crashing onto the pavement. *He'll break his neck,* she thought, *before I have a chance to tell again how much I love him!* She caught hold of Morgan, telling him in that one brief contact that she couldn't wait for Nolan to reach them, and he sent her off with a little shove that said more than anything else could have how heartily he approved.

Somehow her feet were more sure on the ice than they had ever been before, and suddenly it was she who was running. Nolan opened his arms and she slid into them, nearly toppling them both, and then his mouth was there, surrounding hers eagerly.

"I love you!" he declared, and she saw that his nose was turning red and his eyes were shimmering, and she was just bursting with the sheer joy of it. "See that kid over there!" he exclaimed, pointing a gloved finger at Laine, who teetered expectantly on the curb. "That's *my* kid! I don't care who she belonged to before, but that's *my* kid now, and I'm going to marry her mother! You hear that? I'm going to marry her mother!"

He was shouting and hugging her and jabbing at Laine, and then they were slipping and sliding together toward the curb and their daughter. They reached the grass median between the walk and the curb, and he grabbed Laine and lifted her high into the air. She squealed, half with fright and half with amusement at the crazy scene that had just played out before her.

"Hey!" he announced, bringing her down safely into his arms. "I'm going to marry your mother. What d'you think of that?" The dark wispy brows shot up into her hairline.

"Well," she said, just so he'd know what he was getting into, "she's been married before." Nolan laughed, and Mary Judith laughed, and Laine shook her head at them, understanding little of it but liking it and wondering how it had all come about. "Uh-oh." She pointed over Nolan's shoulder, and he turned in time to smile at the officer as he strode up, glowering beneath the visor of his hat, his hobnailed boots making scritching sounds on the ice.

"Okay, buddy," he said, "this'd better be good."

"Oh, it is!" Nolan and Mary Judith answered in tandem. Each looked at the other and tried to suppress widening smiles, while Laine giggled simply for the sheer pleasure of it. Morgan Tanner stepped very cautiously over the sidewalk and came to stand behind them.

"Actually, officer," he announced in his best take-charge voice, "my son has just gotten engaged to be married." As if that explained everything.

"Yes, just," Nolan added.

"This minute," Mary Judith clarified, nodding her head.

"We've been married before," Laine informed him.

The officer stared at the whole lot of them, gave them his best escapee-from-the-booby-hatch glare, and they stood there with their silly smiles pasted on their faces and nodded as if he'd heard the entire story in minute detail. He drew in a deep breath and cleared his throat, ready to throw the book at them, but Morgan stepped forward and began speaking swiftly. Clearly he intended to handle the matter, and Nolan was only too happy to leave it to him.

Nolan turned to Mary Judith, noticing from the corner of his eye that his father had dispatched his driver to move the sports car.

"Well, if you didn't know before you surely know now what kind of fool you're getting for a husband. And the sad part is, Judith, I knew all along. I knew this was where I belonged, and that thing I was working for, that murky, mysterious thing, do you know what it was? I do. I know now. Approval." He turned his gaze on his father, still talking and gesturing and nodding to the policeman. His shoulders were slightly rounded and stooped, not so much that anyone who hadn't lived with a vision of him standing upright and ramrod straight would have noticed. But Nolan noticed and was saddened by the sight and yet strangely gladdened, too. "I guess what I was really after was my father's approval," he said. "And all along I had it." He turned his gaze back to her, and it was so full of love, so full of wanting that she had to fight back the tears. "I had it all along," he whispered, "and I didn't know!"

"And how do you feel about that, Nolan?" she asked, trying to reach her arms around him and hug him through the bulk of his coat.

"I can't really say yet," he answered honestly. "All I know is that when I looked back at the three of you standing here, I thought, there is everything I love, everything that really matters to me, and what is it for if it's not for them?"

She buried her face against his chest. "Welcome home," she said. "Welcome home."

He tilted her head back then and kissed her, and when he lifted his face from hers his father had made his way across the frozen street again and was slowly approaching.

"My driver's taken your car around the block," he said. "When he gets back, I'm going to have him take me on to Dallas. You two have plans to make. Oh, and about the other, there'll be a fine to pay, I'm afraid, but I wouldn't worry about it. There was no damage done."

"Thank you," Judith said, turning to stand with her arm about Nolan's waist. "Thank you for everything, Morgan."

He shook his head. "No, no, I should be thanking you. You're what will make my son happy, as his mother made me happy, though I've no doubt he'll be a better husband than I was. He's a better man." He looked away then, his eyes squinting against the harsh morning light. "Well, I'll wait in the car. You two get on with it." He trudged slowly toward the limousine, his head down, and Mary Judith looked up at Nolan, whose hand rested possessively on her shoulder.

He stood there for a moment, watching the old man pick his way across the ice, then he glanced down at her, a question in his eyes. She smiled encouragingly.

"I want to make love to you," he said quietly, and she nodded.

"Soon. We'll make it soon. And forever, darling. We'll make it forever."

He smiled, then lifted a hand and called out, "Dad!" Morgan stopped and turned. "We need to talk," said Nolan. "Let's go inside."

For a long moment father and son stared at each other. Mary Judith tightened her hold on Nolan, praising him for the loving and honorable man he was, then Laine was there, the spectacle all finished, and the four of them skated with tiny, tandem steps up the slippery walk.

Nolan paused at the door and let the others file inside, then he smiled to himself, thinking of the first day he had walked up these steps and opened this door. *If this was my house,* he had thought. No. No, Mary Judith wasn't the sort to hold anything back, she had given him not just her love, but a home and a family and a reason for it all—perhaps even a father. He had come here broken and penniless and all but defeated, and in the months since then he had worked with more determination and force than he ever had before, but it was not that which had made him rich. It was a woman with the power to turn his world upside down and inside out and backward. For all his effort, for all his determination, it took a woman and her special kind of love to make him a truly wealthy man, and he knew that without her and the family she had given him, he would be a poor man, indeed.

READERS' COMMENTS ON
SILHOUETTE ROMANCES:

"The best time of my day is when I put my children to bed at naptime and sit down to read a Silhouette Romance. Keep up the good work."

P.M.*, Allegan, MI

"I am very fond of the quality of your Silhouette Romances. They are so real. I have tried to read some of the other romances, but I always come back to Silhouette."

C.S., Mechanicsburg, PA

"I feel that Silhouette Books offer a wider choice and/or variety than any of the other romance books available."

R.R., Aberdeen, WA

"I have enjoyed reading Silhouette Romances for many years now. They are light and refreshing. You can always put yourself in the main characters' place, feeling alive and beautiful."

J.M.K., San Antonio, TX

"My boyfriend always teases me about Silhouette Books. He asks me, how's my love life and naturally I say terrific, but I tell him that there is always room for a little more romance from Silhouette."

F.N., Ontario, Canada

*names available on request

Take 4
Silhouette Special Edition novels
FREE...

and preview
future
books
in your
home for
15 days!

Start with 4 FREE books, yours to keep. Then, preview 6 brand-new Special Edition® novels—delivered right to your door every month—as soon as they are published.

When you decide to keep them, pay just $1.95 each ($2.50 each in Canada), *with no shipping, handling, or other additional charges of any kind!*

Romance *is* alive, well and flourishing in the moving love stories presented by Silhouette Special Edition. They'll awaken your desires, enliven your senses, and leave you tingling all over with excitement. In each romance-filled story you'll live and breathe the emotions of love and the satisfaction of romance triumphant.

You won't want to miss a single one of the heart-felt stories presented by Silhouette Special Edition; and when you take advantage of this special offer, you won't have to.

You'll also receive a FREE subscription to the Silhouette Books Newsletter as long as you remain a member. Each lively issue is filled with news on upcoming titles, interviews with your favorite authors, even their favorite recipes.

To become a home subscriber and receive your first 4 books FREE, fill out and mail the coupon today!

Silhouette Special Edition®

Silhouette Romance

COMING NEXT MONTH

AFTER THE MUSIC—Diana Palmer
Rock singer Sabina Cane had been warned that Hamilton Thorndon was a formidable man, but nothing could have prepared her for the impact he would have on her life.

FAMILY SECRETS—Ruth Langan
Who was blackmailing Trudy St. Martin? Caine St. Martin and Ivy Murdock joined forces to discover the culprit's identity, and in the process they discovered the secrets of love.

THE HIGHEST TOWER—Ann Hurley
BeeGee was fearless enough to join the Greenings in their work as steeplejacks, but when her heart started falling for Dan Greening she became determined to keep her feet firmly on the ground.

HEART SHIFT—Glenda Sands
Arson...someone had burned down Chris's shop. Chris felt lucky that handsome and imposing Ian West was on the case, until he told her that she was the prime suspect.

THE CATNIP MAN—Barbara Turner
Julia treated life as a serious matter until, aboard a Mississippi riverboat, she met Chad. His infectious good nature chipped away at her reserve and brought laughter and love to her heart.

MINE BY WRITE—Marie Nicole
Professor Kyle McDaniels gladly offered to help Mindy Callaghan with her writing, yet when it came to offering his heart, he was the one who needed a little help.

AVAILABLE NOW:

WRITTEN ON THE WIND
Rita Rainville

GILDING THE LILY
Emilie Richards

KINDRED HEARTS
Lacey Springer

EYE OF THE BEHOLDER
Charlotte Nichols

NOW OR NEVER
Arlene James

CHRISTMAS MASQUERADE
Debbie Macomber